THE MAN FROM
CHINNAMASTA

SELECT KATHA TITLES

THE MAN FROM CHINNAMASTA

Indira Goswami

Translated from the Asomiya
by Prashant Goswami

KATHA

First published by Katha in 2006

Copyright © Katha, 2006

Copyright © for the original
held by the author.

Copyright © for the English translation
rests with KATHA.

KATHA
A3, Sarvodaya Enclave
Sri Aurobindo Marg, New Delhi 110 017

Phone: (91-11) 4141 6600, 4141 6610

Fax: (91-11) 2651 4373

E-mail: marketing@katha.org

Website: http://www.katha.org

KATHA is a registered nonprofit organization
devoted to enhancing the joy of reading.
KATHA VILASAM is its story research and resource centre.

Cover Design: Geeta Dharmarajan
Cover Painting: Tyeb Mehta

Typeset in 11 on 15.5pt Agaramond at Katha

Katha regularly plants trees to replace the wood used in the making of its books.

ISBN 978-81-89020-38-5

First Reprint 2012, Second Reprint 2016

The Brahmaputra trailed across its misty coverlet – white against dappled white. Mighty shanks striped silver, a leucoderma victim, nuzzling at a widowed mother's breast. Seuli flowers cast forth their distracted fragrance to soften the raw odour of butchered flesh. A hushed whisper of dewdrops brushed the kendur shrubs, the round flat outenga leaves that snakehooded them, the ripple-leaved ashoka, the vast khokan.

From the little white temple of Bhuvaneshwari tucked into the heights of the Kamakhya Hills, Chhinnamasta Jatadhari, the ascetic with the matted locks, walked down to the early morning river. He stooped to touch earth and water in prayer. Time passed. Had he bathed already? Had he offered prayers? In that smoky haze, no one knew. Softly the hymns drifted in – homage to the sixty four goddesses, ... O Mother, Violent and Impetuous One, O Golden Goddess ... Raudri, Indrani, goddess of wrath, ever-youthful Mother of all, Vaishnavi ... Durga, Narasinghee, Chamunda ...

The sixty four names of the divine yoginis spilled over, seeping into every nook and cranny of the Nilachal Hills, like fragments of enchanted music.

Unhurriedly, the jatadhari rose from the mist, much like an ancient landmass arising from the water, covered by an assortment of moss, creepers and grass. A fine patina appeared to have settled on his skin, rather like that on ancient bones dug from the deepest caverns of the earth. Perhaps the scorching sun, the searing winds, the bone-chilling winters, the torrential showers he had lived through had left their mark. Or maybe, he was simply uncaring about his person. The dreadlocks were tinged russet. The piercing eyes were sunk deep in their sockets. No one could look him in the eye for long. Where his gaze rested, it set off an eerie shuddering trill, as would a jab from a sharp dagger tip.

It was late October. His disciples waited, some in shawls of soft endi silk, some in warmer wraps. Yet only a few looked up as he walked briskly past, scattering shards of water from his glistening body, to disappear into his cave.

As usual, Ratnadhar had meticulously laid out everything for the morning prayers – tender sprigs of durba grass, blood red hibiscus flowers, sandalwood. He was the eldest son of Manomohan Sarma, renowned priest of the sacred Kamakhya mutt, an important shakti peeth. He had grown up hearing of its consequence from his father: Sati, the incarnation of Parvati – she who is worshipped both as mother and as symbol of erotic love – once lived here with Shiva. She had married Shiva against the wishes of her father, Raja Daksha. And now, unable to bear her father's taunts – the way he called her husband a beggar, a haunter of shamshans – she could do no less than throw herself on his yagna fire. This is the land that her distraught lover walked, her corpse slung across his shoulder, refusing to let her go. And this, the exact spot where the great goddess's vagina, her yoni fell, after Vishnu in his great mercy decimated her body into fifty one pieces. Fifty one places to worhip the goddess, fifty one shakti peeths, Sarma would murmur, but this is the most holy. Because Sati's sacred yoni fell here.

Ratnadhar was an artist. He had a loyal following among the disciples. Delicate hands. A trim figure. A finely chiselled nose. The crown of thick black hair complemented his aristocratic bearing. About a year ago, it was said, he had lost his mind. No doctor, north or south, could cure him. None but Chhinnamasta Jatadhari. And Ratnadhar took up his brush again. He soon became the ascetic's most ardent disciple.

And now, as was his practice every morning, Chhinnamasta Jatadhari sat before the altar, his eyes closed, his fingers tracing gestures in the air. Then, with a deep murmur of "Bhairav! Bhairav!" invoking the fearful form of Shiva, he gathered his palms in the turtle shape, the yoni mudra. Ratnadhar watched in awe. Everyone knew that the secret yoni mudra must never be revealed. It is the very absolute, representing consciousness, granting liberation. At last, from somewhere deep within the jatadhari: "Hram. Hreem. Hraum." Each of these seed mantras corresponded to an aspect of the great goddess. Together the sounds represented all of divinity.

But to which deity had he offered his prayers? No one knew. Not even his favourite disciple, Ratnadhar.

The jatadhari broke the early morning veneration with a loud mouthful of water from the small pitcher at his side. He drew the young disciple to him, fingers grazing his hair in blessing.

Then, brusquely, he turned from the devotees and walked away, Ratnadhar following close behind.

The last few days had been special for Ratnadhar. Chhinnamasta Jatadhari had lately been encouraging the young artist to paint something quite unusual. Paint Captain Welsh arriving with his troops at the steps of Kamakhya, he had said. Paint the huge army of six battalions led by the Captain, to free Gauhati from the Burmese who had infiltrated the eastern borders and overrun the territory for years. It was a time when Kamarupa was a prosperous kingdom, famous for her textiles, sandal and aloe. Situated on the trading route between south China and India, her regional trade was at its peak when Captain Welsh had led the British expedition to Assam in 1792.

To his devotees, Chhinnamasta Jatadhari was a conundrum. His knowledge of history was extensive, the languages he knew were many. This only fuelled the wild speculation that swirled around him. Stories about his origin were perpetually in circulation. Some claimed he was a brilliant scholar form Benaras. Others believed he had been educated in the Tanjore district of South India. Still others had no doubt that he originally belonged to the Trihut region of Bihar.

A follower awaiting the jatadhari's divine audience said aloud as he passed: "Only the other day, a hanged convict's family left the body on the sands of the Brahmaputra. Chhinnamasta Jatadhari prayed continuously for two nights squatting over the corpse. I saw it with my own eyes. If the family abandoned the corpse so, it was only because they wanted the jatadhari to perform the last rites."

"People claim that he crawls into the bellies of dead elephants to meditate," another murmured.

"Eesh!"

A third chimed in. "That's nothing. Stop by the river, on the night after the full moon ..."

"After the full moon?"

The crowd turned eagerly to the speaker.

"Be sure to stand on the battle rock. Yes, that same rock on which the people of Nilachal stood to watch the battle on the Brahmaputra play out. The time the Mughals, at the height of their power, took it on themselves to crush the Ahom king. Take your position I say, even if you must do so seventeen times, as the Mughuls did in 1667. You will witness an amazing sight. No, not Lachit Barphukan the great Ahom general who has been immortalized for the defeat of the Mughuls at Saraighat – but a king cobra! Yes, you'll see the deadly serpent with its hood flared, glistening in the water."

Someone whispered, "That's no snake. It's the jatadhari's dreadlocks. He meditates under water."

"So I've heard. People say he has snakes entangled in his hair."

Bom Bom Shiva! Bom Raudra!
Bom Bom Bom Shiva Shambhu!
Shiva Shambhu!

Startled, the disciples looked up. Even those who were resting, their weary heads tucked between their knees. Two saffron clad hermits made a dramatic entry. One was tall, the other abnormally short. Matted hair bunched into top-knots, rudraksh beads prominent on their necks, wooden water pots held high. Probably newcomers to Nilachal.

Just then, Ratnadhar screamed, gesticulating at the buffalo they were leading to the sacrificial altar. He threw himself down, scrabbling frantically at the earth, flecks of foam gathering at the corners of his mouth. "Stop! Stop! Don't you see? It's terrified, it doesn't want to go with you. See how it defecates in fear. Look at its eyes. Have some mercy on the beast. It wants to live and play on Ma's Earth. Stop I say! Stop!"

The clicking of hooves splintered into a hundred pieces. Khat, Khat, Khat, Kharat. Khat, Khat, Kharang, Kharat. Driving the onlookers to silence.

Suddenly a murmur rose. The hoofbeats pounded hard in Ratnadhar's chest, the eddies of sound coursing through his body like hot blood. He beat at the ground with his fists. The crowd grew.

The ascetic from Chhinnamasta cut through the surging mass of devotees – the asthma victims, the deranged, the gastric patients, the fathers of marriageable daughters. Gently, he took Ratnadhar and eased him to the ground. The bystanders closed in to get a better look. The jatadhari was squatting over the young man, in meditation, chanting Om Hreeng ... Om Hreeng. His voice was soft, mesmerizing. One by one, he picked up the flowers and offered them in concentrated worship as he repeated the incantations. He brought both his hands to his chest then, taking the hibiscus blooms from the copper plate, he touched one to his forehead, the other to Ratnadhar's.

"Ma Chhinnamasta! Ma Chhinnamasta!"

It was a long while before he opened his eyes and looked up at the crowd.

Immediately there was a small stampede.

They heard footsteps. It was a man and a woman, wrapped snugly in shawls, walking towards the ascetic. No one could immediately recognize them. The woman slipped off her shawl. And there was a frozen moment of silence. Then, a rippling murmur: Who is she? Where is she from?

All eyes turned towards her. A white woman. Her auburn hair cascaded below her shoulders. She wore her long skirt much like a mekhela, as any other Assamese woman would, with a woollen blouse. Her chest heaved like the fluttering wings of a dove being taken to the sacrificial altar.

Foreigner?

Yes, yes. Foreigner.

Not that this was the first time a foreigner from across the seven seas had come to the holy abode. It was the 1920s after all.

Chhinnamasta Jatadhari cried out, "Ma! Ma! Ma Chhinnamasta!"

Loud silence. Then the devotees chorused, "Ma! Ma!"

The munshi's hair was long, his teeth stuck out. He took off his turban as he pushed his way through the gathering, to fall at the ascetic's feet.

"O Yogi, I have brought a memsahib with me. Forgive me if I have sinned. She is a very unhappy woman."

A concerned voice asked, "Has she entered any of the temples? Of Bhuvaneshwari? Bhairavi? Chhinnamasta, Bhumawati, Bagala, Kali, Tara?"

The munshi vigorously shook his head.

"No, no. Dorothy memsahib even took off her shoes before she came to this place. She bowed in reverence before stepping out on this sacred pilgrimage."

The jatadhari opened his eyes. His voice was grave, "Who is she? Where is she from?"

Folding his palms, the munshi said obsequiously, "She has come to you with great hope."

Everyone in the audience raised their heads for another look. Her eyes, luminous as the waters of the Brahmaputra, reflected the winter skies ... Or, did they hide the scars of past turmoil? Her complexion was pale like a skinned gourd. Her gaze, soft as a water ripple, betrayed a pain so intense, it evoked heartfelt sympathy. Anyone would want to share in her pain, her torment, and ask, "What happened? What's wrong?"

Chhinnamasta Jatadhari signalled her with his eyes to come closer. As she stepped forward, her feet were visible. The jatadhari motioned her to be seated. A disciple sprang up to spread a straw mat.

Amazing! She was a white woman, but so different from the Europeans they had seen on the streets of Gauhati. None of them had this kind of hair. The coppery tint matched the colour of the sacrificial machetes so perfectly. Her eyes could be compared to the water-pits inside the temple, glittering in the flickering light of the earthen lamps.

The jatadhari closed his eyes and meditated for a while. Then, "Ma! Ananga-kusuma protect the space before me. Ananga-mekhala protect from behind. On the left, Ananga-madana protect me ... Ananga-rekha always, and forever, shield me from above. Ananga-kusha always protect me from all directions! Ma! Ma!" In a trance, he slipped off his seat, rocking back and forth, his eyes fixed on the temple, his palms touching his forehead in salutation – "Ma! I take refuge at your feet, absolve me of my sins of the last seven births.

Ma! Ma sapta-janma-arjitat papat,
trahi maam sharanegatam."

The front rows parted to make way. Composed at last, he rose, as if awakening from a deep sleep. He looked straight at the woman in front of him. Then he turned towards the munshi and said, "Ask her to speak in front of everyone. In her heart sits the king with the crown of thorns. Why then has she come here?"

The woman's lips quivered, her eyes brimmed over as she turned to the munshi.

Chhinnamasta Jatadhari repeated his question.

The munshi glanced at her. She seemed to give him her assent.

"Reverend one, her name is Dorothy. Dorothy Brown, the wife of Henry Brown, principal of Cotton College."

This time the audience curiously scrutinized the woman. The principal's wife from Cotton College? The college wasn't very old but it was already famous. It had been founded by Sir Henry Cotton in Gauhati in 1901.

Dorothy undid the scarf from around her neck and tried to tie up her unruly hair. Prespiration beaded her forehead.

"What does she want to say?" the ascetic sounded impatient.

Silence. A little bird passed overhead, fluttering in the stillness.

One by one, more devotees trickled in. They all sat in rapt attention, ready to savour the ascetic's every word, as if it were old wine.

"What have you come to seek?"

"Peace of mind."

"Peace of mind?"

The words purled from Chhinnamasta Jatadhari's mouth. "No peace of mind, no peace of mind!" He raised his hands sharply, asking the crowd. "Do any of you have peace of mind?"

No one replied. Not even the man who, till a while ago, had been dominating the gathering. The ascetic allowed himself a smile. He said in a consoling voice, "No one is happy. No one.

People somehow manage to string body and soul together and carry on."

The woman tried to say something but no one could decipher her words. Only the jatadhari perhaps understood that she was trying to tell him that all her efforts always seemed to crumble to dust.

The munshi came to her aid, saying, "If your grace would permit Dorothy memsahib a private audience ... she wishes to become your disciple."

The jatadhari hesitated. Then, without a word, he rose and strode majestically off towards Bhuvaneshwari. He walked blindly like a wild elephant that crushes everything in its path. Some devotees trailed after him. Dorothy stood with the munshi under the gamble tree, bewildered.

After a while, the jatadhari returned. The faithful waited eagerly – would the jatadhari grant Dorothy a personal audience in his cave?

The clack of wooden sandals.

All eyes turned towards the cleanshaven, saffron robed hermit who earlier lived on the banks of Torsa, Coochbehar. Dark and ugly, the sacred thread flapping across his chest like dried animal guts. He had come during Ambubachi, the annual utsav when the temple is closed for four days because the goddess is believed to be going through her menstrual period. The hermit from the banks of the Torsa had stayed on in the Bhairavi temple premises since one such Ambubachi. Bhairavi was ever on his lips – salutations to Goddess Tripura Bhairavi, the embodiment of compassion, the abode of peace, the manifestation of the supreme soul in the form of sound. *Mahapadma-anantasthi karunananda vigraha, Sabd-brahmamaye swasti bande tripurari bhairavim.* Pointing an accusing finger at the jatadhari, the hermit from Torsa rasped, "It is forbidden for an untouchable to become a disciple."

"Disciple? Untouchable?" The jatadhari roared. "I do not have disciples. I do not initiate anyone. I live in total solitude." He sighed deeply, then continued, "But I am aware of the five rules of initiation: Do not initiate a sinner, an evil-doer, a person with no respect for mantra, a person with no respect for a teacher, and one with a stained soul."

The hermit from Torsa took one step forward, "Do not initiate the lazy, the enraged, those with unaccounted wealth, beggars, or those proud of their knowledge. Differentiate not between man and woman. Those who come to me seeking solace are the wretched and the ignorant."

The sound of buffalo hooves rose over the verbal duel between the jatadhari and the hermit. The animal tried to break free as it was being hauled away to the slaughterhouse. It wanted to escape the death that came in the form of pilgrims. But the harbingers of doom kept tugging at it. Shoving. Yelling. Prodding.

Ratnadhar still lay limp on the ground. The ascetic lifted him in his arms and looked towards the temple. "Ma! Ma! Ma Chhinnamasta! Ma Chhinnamasta! Ma! Ma!"

Someone threw a stone. But the stone did not touch the jatadhari. None could comprehend what suddenly came over Dorothy. She ripped through the crowd and flung herself at the jatadhari's feet, sobbing uncontrollably.

The munshi, nonplussed, said, "It is time for the master to return from the college. The buggy must have stopped in front of the gate."

The hermit from Torsa wagged a warning finger at the swarm of devotees in front of the jatadhari's dwelling: "What are you doing? The woman will now enter the abode. I know all about the jatadhari's experiments. He will disrobe this white devotee to test his shakta skills on her. Get up and do something ... do something."

The tension mounted. Still nobody moved. "I know. He will have to touch her yoni for his experiments ..."

Suddenly, two devotees leapt up and grabbed the hermit by the arms. He struggled to free himself. A loud crash interrupted them. The buffalo had freed itself from its tormentors. It charged straight into the gathering. In the chaos that ensued, the crowd scattered, everyone running helter-skelter. But Dorothy Brown stood frozen under the tree, a mute witness as a devotee was gored to death by the horns of the stampeding buffalo.

The boat sloshed through the water, to the shore. Munshi Vepin Chandra got off. He looked back at the mighty Brahmaputra — just where it veered off its course, to take the shape of a sacrificial machete. The waters had receded around Urvasi, an island in the river, revealing carvings of Vishnu in his half-lion form, the Narasimha avatar. A strip of sand also lay exposed, like the pelt of a white goat laid out to dry after the sacrifice.

Arrangements had already been made for Dorothy Brown at Darbhanga House, the solid ancient construction that had withstood the test of time. Though everybody knew the house by that name, no one could recall whether it had actually been constructed by the Darbhanga King of Mithila or a devotee of the Mother.

The munshi had brought along an army of workers, including a carpenter. They unloaded sacks, bags and trunks. Two men carried the bags of cement and sand up the slope. A kitchen had already been designated in the dilapidated house. A stove, utensils, crockery – everything was unpacked. The wise munshi had thought of everything. But vestiges of the past remained. Previously, ascetics from Trihut, Madhupur, North Kanshi, Nawadwip and, even from the far off Himalayas, converged at the temple around August-September for Manasa puja, when the snake goddess is ceremoniously worshipped. They took shelter in Darbhanga House, and had all but wrecked it in the process. The rooms were littered with earthen pots, wooden sandals, pieces of saffron cloth, shards of hookah bowls and dried up sweetmeats. Petrified excreta, human or animal – god only knew – had left stubborn stains on the floor.

The men set down the luggage and came outside. On the broken-down veranda, an emaciated workman looked at the gamble trees that skirted the house. "This house is surely haunted," he said. "Let me start by cutting away some branches, so that memsahib can soak in the beauty of the Brahmaputra. Look! You can see the Sukreshwar bathing banks from here – Lord Brahmaputra has really been eating up the shoreline. What's that floating away? Seems like a whole forest!"

The munshi was growing impatient. "Come on, get going. Start off with the door frame."

The men poured out the sand and cement, noisily churning them into mortar. The carpenter went off to lop off some branches before settling down with his tools to repair the broken doorframe.

By evening, they had managed to carve out a bathroom and a bedroom from the ruins. The munshi even hung curtains in the bedroom to discourage inquisitive passers-by. The Brahmaputra was clearly visible from the veranda, now that the trees had had their branches pruned.

The sky had gathered up a coverlet of clouds. The mighty Brahmaputra flowed silently beneath it, like some ancient bark of the sanchi tree. Munshi Vepin Chandra smiled contentedly. Yes, he told himself, Now memsahib can bask in the glory of the Brahmaputra. She can entertain all the gora sahibs she pleases. If need be, she could even hold discourses with the jatadhari here. The foreigners would never venture onto the temple premises. But, wouldn't it be convenient for them to cross the river and come directly up to this house? Who knows? The other day, Brown sahib lost his temper and whipped the carriage driver for some trivial misdemeanour. Who knows what the future holds?

Within a week the house was habitable. And on a full moon night in mid-January, Dorothy Brown disembarked from the boat firmly clutching the hand of the faithful Munshi Vepin. A mantle of fog shimmered like silver dust over the leaf littered abode of the Mother Goddess – much like scrapings from the silver pot used to make offerings of sacrificial blood to the goddess. And there was the Brahmaputra. In silent repose.

A pack of jackals howled, and swiftly crossed their path to melt into the thicket. Dorothy Brown walked briskly with the munshi, a harried servant carrying her trunk followed behind. This path was now familiar to the munshi. He had travelled by it many a time in the last few days. The munshi had been helpful, sticking out his neck with his superiors regarding Dorothy's decision to stay in this abandoned house – a haven for stray dogs and jackals, cattle and horses not to mention godmen. But he had argued persuasively on the memsahib's behalf and had finally triumphed. No wonder the valley people compared him with the famous Revenue Supervisor Harakanta who had been a great favourite of the Ahom King as well as with the Britishers.

The munshi wiped the glass-chimney with his hands and lit the kerosene lamp. He made Dorothy's bed and set up the mosquito net, taking the trouble to tuck in the edges. When at last it was time to leave, he said, "Brown sahib has sent the watchman, Parashuram, to stay here. He will be sleeping in the room next to yours. I would have asked him to stay outside in the veranda, but it is very cold. The wind from the Brahmaputra would freeze him. Do you mind?"

Dorothy Brown was busy settling in. She said, "I shall stay alone."

"The master insisted ..." The clerk said apologetically. "There are wild animals in the vicinity. You saw the jackals that crossed us on our way this evening. Parashuram is a faithful old servant. Let him stay."

Dorothy Brown gave the munshi a stern look. "From now on, I have nothing whatsoever to do with your master. I shall decide what is best for my own welfare and honour. I will send Parashuram back in the morning. Tell your master he is never to try and visit me here."

The old munshi pulled a handkerchief from his pocket and wiped his face. "There's a lot to think about. The night itself will teach you many things and make you as wise as the sea."

It was quite late by the time he took leave of his mistress to climb down the slope. The moon lit up the dirt road leading to the river. An eerie calm seemed to have descended on the Brahmaputra. The shivering boatmen were waiting for the munshi. Oars splashed in the water as they sailed away.

It was early dawn when Dorothy suddenly woke up. She pulled aside the mosquito net. The window over her bed was slightly ajar. Sleepily she stumbled to it. The Brahmaputra! But what was that floating by in the murky light? Some ancient temple? A whole forest of trees?

Suddenly, something rustled outside.

"Who ...? Who's there?" Dorothy peered out into the half light, suddenly afraid. She could make out a figure standing under the gamble tree. She strained her eyes to get a better look. It was the hermit from Torsa.

What was *he* doing here at *this* hour of the night? "Parashu! Parashu!" She shouted. At once the hermit vanished into the night.

By morning, the news had spread that Dorothy Brown had come to live in the abode of the Mother Goddess. By the time the munshi arrived, a group of idlers had already assembled. A few had even shinned up the jamun tree. Lewd whistles and catcalls came from its branches.

"The jatadhari will get a taste of the memsahib."

"He will ask her to put on the mahasankhamala for the fulfilment of her desires."

"What are you saying?"

"Yes, yes. She will have to wear the garland of bones."

"But, where will he find so many skull bones to make the garland?"

"Dig around in his dreadlocks and you'll find them. Everyone knows."

Splash. Splash. Splash. A boat.

The two youngsters, hanging like monkeys from the trees, jumped down and pranced merrily down the slope. Perhaps they'd get a ride to Gauhati on the boat.

The jatadhari sat on a mat in front of Dorothy. The munshi placed a wooden stool before him, then went out onto the veranda, to squat there with his head between his knees. His hair was all white. So were his eyebrows. He wore gold earrings like most elderly Assamese people. Loose folds of skin rippled below his eyes and chin.

A few young men were still loitering around Darbhanga House. Leaning against a column, Munshi Vepin cast a quick look around, making a mental note to tell the jatadhari all he knew.

"Memsahib didn't know that Brown sahib was involved with a Khasi woman. She found the letters, photographs and drawings when she came back unexpectedly from London."

"Letters, photographs and drawings?"

"Yes. Memsahib was away for a year. She had gone to London for medical treatment."

"Treatment?"

"Yes, holy one! She has no children."

The jatadhari was silent. He looked up at Dorothy. Her pallor seemed to increase. Intense emotions flickered across her face, but no words came. Even so, all her thoughts seemed to flow straight to the jatadhari's heart. It was long past the time for prayer.

He rose abruptly and walked over to the temple of Chhinnamasta. Inside, he located an old crate hidden in its dark recesses, and took out a garland that lay entwined in a string of rudraksha beads. Returning a while later, he found Dorothy still sitting there, absorbed in the Brahmaputra.

"This is the mahasankhamala," he said, looking at her. "It has been made with the bones taken from the forehead of a human skull – the bridge between the nose and the eyes, known as mahasankha.

Ma, Ma Chhinnamasta! Ma! Ma!" He paused, then added, "And the rudraksha, I am sure you know. When Shiva saw the cruelty on earth, he wept. Trees sprouted where his tears fell. The seeds from those trees are called rudraksha or god's teardrops. It is said that those who wear these beads need no longer weep because Shiva weeps for them.

Dorothy Brown shivered. The munshi went to stand by her side. He could clearly see a vein throbbing under the delicate skin of her temples.

The jatadhari completed his rituals at the temple of Chhinnamasta and left for his own cave. Like every other day, women had gathered there, most of them with their heads covered with the achal, the edge, of their chadars. Tall, short, fat, thin – the jatadhari counted eight women, one with a baby in her arms, whose achal kept slipping off as the baby suckled. Every time she tried to pull it back, her shapely nose and full fruit bud lips became visible.

A few idlers had taken up their usual places on the tree and the rocks. They knew the best branches and the right hollows in which to position themselves for the best view of the jatadhari's activities. There was always a scuffle for the vantage point and today as usual, the pushing and shoving had started.

One by one, the women entered the sinister darkness of the ascetic's cave. Sometimes, a limb would flash from the shadowy depths. Every woman who emerged had pulled up her chadar to cover her head.

Oars splashed in the distance. This time a woman alighted from the boat, hitching up her mekhela. Her hair was tied into a large knot held together with hairpins. She was wearing a muga silk mekhela with a cotton chadar, with a coloured puff sleeved blouse made of coarse cotton cloth. She had her ten year old son in tow. The naughty boy would probably have fallen into the river, had she not held tightly onto his hand. The mother did not let go of her boy for an instant.

She was followed by an elderly man with grey hair. His grimy dhuti stopped short of his knees. A cotton chadar covered his almost bare body. A cord was tied around his neck – the kind used for tying cattle. He did not utter a word. Did not reply when questioned. He just mooed like a cow. He had come to collect alms in order to find salvation. There was no mistake – he had killed a cow. He had to now atone for his sin by begging for alms with a rope tied around his neck for twelve long years.

But had he killed the animal deliberately? Or had it been an accident? The bystanders asked, their eyes full of pity as the three walked up to the jatadhari.

The front of the cave was already crowded with women waiting to pour out their woes to the ascetic. A mere touch would perhaps redeem ... a mere touch ... a few specks of dust from his feet ... But the pretty light skinned woman with the boy caused a stir. All eyes turned towards her as she raised her hands skywards, imploring loudly: "Hear me, O reverend one, help me! It happened this morning."

The devotees cried out, "What happened?"

"My son was playing with his friends in the sands where the sahibs practice shooting."

A voice interjected, "That's not a good place. The sahibs hang grapefruit up as shooting targets. If anyone dares to go and watch them, they kick them out with their boots."

"He tripped on something under the dangling fruits."

The jatadhari asked, "What thing?"

The woman twisted her fingers a bit, silent. Then looking him in the eye said, "A skull."

"Skull?"

A gasp from the onlookers.

The woman continued, "It looked like a human skull. Quite large and irregular."

"Irregular?"

"Yes."

A wave of whispering washed over the crowd: "It must have been a skull that had been offered to Ma."

"Must be a thousand year old offering!"

Someone from the crowd cried out, "Ma Chhinnamasta! Ma! Ma Chhinnamasta!"

The others joined him, "Ma! Ma! Ma!"

The woman with the child was on the verge of tears. She was trembling, fearful that some inauspicious star would cast its evil spell on her son who had played football with the skull. The jatadhari rose from his seat. There was a long silence as he gazed at the Brahmaputra. He turned to the woman, and said in a soothing tone, "Child! A child can't be blamed. Ma! Ma! Ma Chhinnamasta! Ma! Ma! Read the seventy sixth chapter of the *Kalika Purana* that contains the rules and rituals of worship of the Goddess Shakti and promotes the vedas.

"The person to be sacrificed must bathe properly. Eat only boiled vegetarian food the night before, and abstain from physical association. He is elaborately dressed, with ornaments, and smears his forehead with sandalwood paste. He must be seated facing the north, along with the deities, and then worshipped: Brahma the creator will be worshipped on his navel. The earth, on his nose. The fire god, Agni, on the tongue.

Enlightenment, in his eyes. Strength and the sky, on his ears."

He paused. "You all know that the spot where the severed head of a sacrificed human or animal falls indicates the fortune, good or bad, that will visit the one who offers the sacrifice."

One of the devotees shouted, "O Reverend Jatadhari, tell us – if you have seen a human sacrifice performed?"

The jatadhari raised his hands to the devotees, and with his eyes closed, repeated the name of the goddess over and over again. A film of perspiration glossed his nose, which the divine sculptor seemed to have shaped like Lord Vishnu's. He added, "How does the position in which the severed head falls forecast the events to follow? They say that the *Kalika Purana* tells you of the direction that assures wealth or the birth of a male child. If the severed head falls in the north-east, the king will be overthrown. If the severed head clatters its teeth, the person offering the sacrifice will certainly fall ill. Listen, it is also clearly stated that should the severed head laugh, fortune will smile on the person offering the sacrifice. The *Kalika Purana* even claims that the last words spoken by the sacrificed victim always come true. If the severed head grunts, then the country will surely be reduced to dust."

The woman who was listening to the jatadhari in rapt attention asked tremulously, "What am I supposed to do now?"

"Mai, believe me, these are ancient writings and beliefs. You can no longer smell sacrificed limbs burning in the sacrificial fires, can you? Can anyone today stand for a whole day and night before the Mother, holding an oil lamp in the severed head of a sacrificed buffalo? The sacred bowls in which blood and lotus flowers were offered to the Mother have all disappeared. Today this terrible history has been confined to the deep recesses of dark caves. We will bury this past in a tomb of flowers."

The woman stood there, hesitating. Tears rolled down her cheeks. The assembled devotees felt sorry for her. A harassed mother, unable to marry off her daughter said, "Go up to the jatadhari and he'll teach you how to absolve the evil of his deed."

The woman pressed forward. The jatadhari stared into her eyes, his gaze so sharp, she felt it would rip her apart. Quickly, she lowered her eyes, kneeling to touch his feet. The jatadhari touched her head and said gently, "There is nothing to fear. What proof have you that it was a skull from a sacrifice that was accepted by the goddess?"

The woman pulled her son forward, telling him to touch the jatadhari's feet and seek his blessings. But the boy held back. They were interrupted by a scream. A woman in the front, who had come to seek help to mend her drunken husband's waywardness, made a futile attempt to lose herself among the devotees. The man, pounced on her, and grabbed her by the hair, hurling abuses. "You bitch! You should be pounding the paddy at home. How dare you come to this charlatan who has abducted a foreign woman. You whore!"

B oom. Boom ... boom. The reverberations echoed as far as Bhuvaneshwari. Down below in Kalipur, the Britishers were playing with their guns.

Once, only the chirping parghumas and mynahs came at dusk to feed on the seeds of the seleng trees. Now, dawn broke to the sound of the sahibs' guns. Wild shrubs and evergreens covered the hill, all the way down to the river. Along its banks the smoky blue jacarandas blossomed. This side of Kalipur was the tiger's domain. Their roars were blown across by the winds in the daytime. Officers of the East Bengal Company and the government of Assam went hunting here. The sahibs from the Steamer Company cycled up at dawn for target practice. Many a tree had been felled. Even Captain Welsh and his huge army had not caused so much destruction.

The bullets often missed their targets and hit the nests of tokoras or barhoitokas. Sometimes they got a flapping dhanesh.

On occasion a bird dropped from the sky, landing in the midst of the jatadhari's congregation.

The hopefuls were milling about again today. They had come to meet the jatadhari. Some came by boat. Others had walked all the way. Each was beset by their own share of troubles. Yesterday, the ascetic had been spotted in broad daylight, swimming across to Bhasmachal. The island in the Brahmaputra was famous because of its Jyotirlinga. The wives of the Kamakhya priests had come out in their numbers. In red-bordered sarees and flaring sendur bindis, they stood on the elephant-trunk-rock to watch. They saw the jatadhari standing on the Bhasmachal rocks.

Two women broke unobtrusively away from the group to make a quick run to the Darbhanga House. Quite a crowd was gathered there already. The jatadhari had given Dorothy the mahasankhamala. They were dying to know what it was all about.

What did she do all day behind those shuttered windows?

Two priests who had gone to collect water for puja had caught a glimpse of her at daybreak. In heavy overcoat and woollen cap, she had come down to the riverfront and walked around for a while before hurrying back to the house. The Torsa hermit and the Tibetan monk had also reported seeing her there.

In the mornings, out on her own, she avoided prying eyes. When she sat out on the veranda, she saw nothing but the Brahmaputra.

She has seen the Mother walking on the sacred river. Her third eye has set the waves on fire. The trees on Bhasmachal and the peaks of the distant mountains were aflame. She came down from Nilachal, swift as the wind, trident in hand, a garland of hibiscus round her neck. Her clothes were stained with sacrificial blood, like the magnificent Tripura Bhairavi! Four armed, books in her left hand, the three eyes flashed with the brilliance of a thousand suns. She moved majestically, graceful as an elephant! The great Mother, playing with the river!

William Smith from the Steamer Company had once told Dorothy, "I saw the jatadhari when I took the boat to Amingaon. That man from the temple of Chhinnamasta. One can't look him in the eye. A sort of fire consumes the body. He was floating on the river, the locks spread out. Extraordinary! A poisonous snake was all tangled up in his hair. I saw it with my own eyes. Yellow, with black stripes. A strange poisonous snake twisted happily around his matted locks."

The wives of the priests Rambangshi and Dambaru, approached Dorothy with some caution. Rambangshi's wife asked, "How long will you be staying?"

Dorothy looked up but did not answer.

"Have you left your husband for good?"

Still no answer.

The women whispered to each other: "The jatadhari may have asked her not to speak to anyone from this peeth. Does she know any Asomiya?"

"I'm sure she knows some. All these foreigners in Gauhati are learning Asomiya," retorted Rambangshi's wife. "They even read Asomiya books in the Curzon Hall."

Suddenly Dorothy asked in halting Asomiya, "What happened to your hands? What are those stains?" She sounded concerned.

She could speak some Asomiya. She had picked up a few words from the munshi. Both women slipped their hands into the folds of their sarees. The backs of their palms were all shrivelled up. The skin was coarse and dry.

One of the women took off her achal. "It's because we spend all our lives in the kitchen, cooking."

"Cooking?"

"Yes. If we don't cook for our jajmans – our patrons – who will?"

"Jajmans' meals?"

"Yes, for sixty to eighty people every day."

"Don't they live in guest houses?" Dorothy asked.

The women glanced furtively around. One never knew. Somebody might just see them talking to the foreigner. Only the other day, one of them had overheard her father-in-law remarking to a patron while smoking a hookah on the veranda, "Beware. Don't dare go anywhere near that foreigner. She has been consorting with our jatadhari."

Dorothy vanished into the house and came back with her first-aid box. "Let me put some salve on your hands. I picked up some good ointments from the ship on my last trip home. Come on. Show me your hands ..."

They hesitated. But curiosity soon got the better of them. Just then, the old priest Panchanan Sarma spotted them. Leaning on his cane, he shouted, "What are you up to? You will have to bathe again." At once the women darted off down the dirt lanes, through the shrubbery to their homes. Puzzled, Dorothy closed the box and went inside. She locked the door behind her.

The hermit from Torsa had just bathed in the Brahmaputra. Lurking around the Darbhanga House as usual, he craned his neck, but no it didn't look like Dorothy Brown would come out today.

There was no one about. He put some sendur, turmeric powder and sandalwood paste from the bag on his shoulder into a small copper bowl. Were those the incantations to subjugate, that he muttered under his breath? Or a prayer because he had just bathed?

Oars splashed through the water. Some pilgrims got off the boat chattering loudly. A large man held a three year old child on his right arm, a goat in his left. The child played with the plump stippled male goat. Soon the child's forehead would be smeared with his playmate's blood.

Behind the man walked his wife, her head covered.

The hermit from Torsa blocked their path. Holding out the copper bowl, he asked, "Will you give me blood?"

The goat wriggled, nuzzling its head into the child. The man held on tight.

The hermit was insistent, "Take it. Take the bowl. I need blood."

The wife nervously took the bowl and proceeded.

Jatadhari's voice floated to them from the distance, "Ma! Ma! Ma! Ma Chhinnamasta! Ma."

A buggy stopped at the gates of Kamakhya. Such a splendid brace of black and white horses had never been seen in Gauhati before. They had been brought all the way from Peshawar. There were only three or four of these buggies in Gauhati. One was retained by the foreigners working in the Calcutta based Trail and Company located at 20, British India Street. The British officers of the Great Indian Peninsular Railways also used a similar buggy.

Henry Brown stepped carefully out of the buggy. He was a thick set man. His chest was broad. Not yet forty, he sported a full crown of hair, the colour of a dried honeycomb. His nose was straight, like a Greek god's. His eyes were shrewd. He wore a pair of khaki trousers, a pristine white shirt and a khaki hat.

Henry Brown. He should have been a film star. Each stride had purpose. Munshi Vepin, accompanying his sahib, lifted the corner of his dhuti and trotted behind him, trying to catch up.

Henry was quite used to climbing hills. But today he was panting, agitated. He had to stop once to catch his breath. The munshi took out his handkerchief and tried to fan him with it but Brown waved him off. He took off his hat, trying to cool off. Then he fished out a kerchief from his pocket to mop his face. Palanquin bearers chanted a rhythmic: "Helou Hesou! Helou, Hesou!"

A straggle of people followed the palanquin. It was the sort used for carrying the sick. Henry noticed the man inside was wounded, his clothes were bloodstained.

A priest stopped at the sight of a white man.

"What happened?" the munshi enquired.

"A pilgrim from Coochbehar. His eldest son is sick and he has no money for treatment. Can't afford to sacrifice a goat or a buffalo. So he offered his own blood."

"His own blood?" Brown was astounded.

A helpful voice piped up, "The *Kalika Purana* says that a devotee should not offer more than four times the amount of blood that can be held in a lotus petal. If he had offered a tiny bit of flesh – the size of a sesame seed – from his chest, his prayers would have been answered within six months. The sick child would have recovered by now."

"But ..."

"But?"

"He cut himself with a sharp knife. He had just begun the prayer, O, Mother of the universe, bestower of all worldly desires, be pleased with my offering of drops of blood from my body ... when he passed out."

The palanquin passed. They watched the crowd fade down the hill.

Brown and the munshi resumed their climb. "We should have come by boat and climbed up the other side," the munshi was apologetic. It leads directly up to Darbhanga House. But, please sir, do not worry, sir. I have personally taken care of memsahib's quarters."

His sahib was barely listening. He was growing more and more agitated as they walked. By the time they reached Darbhanga House, the doors and windows of the house had been shut. "Dorothy."

Silence.

"I've come to take you home my dear. You can't live here like this." The munshi considered knocking, but hesitated in deference to his master. Henry Brown called out: "Dorothy ... Dorothy ... Damn these mosquitoes! You'll die from cholera. I've come to take you home. Let's go, darling."

Henry looked down at the Brahmaputra. What was that, riding on its back? The ruins of some ancient temple ... Black waters ... Terrifying. Like corpses carried away in the jaws of death.

"Dorothy, listen to me. This is not the place for you. They're different, these people, please try and understand." He cajoled through the door, "Things are going from bad to worse these days. They dragged your friend Smith off his horse the other day and gave him a sound thrashing. Haven't you heard?"

"It's true memsahib, what sahib says." The old clerk as always supported his master. "This place is not safe for you. There's trouble brewing. The Simon Commission is due to sit at Pandu in January ... we have heard that some Cotton College students are ready with sticks ... they found a gun in the students' hostel only last night ... please open the door memsahib."

No. Dorothy would not open the door.

Brown's temper boiled over. "Come on out you stupid cow!" He burst out, kicking at the door, hammering at it with his fists. The munshi went round the back to see if a door or window had been left open by chance. By now an audience of devotees and ascetics from the neighbourhood had collected, spellbound by the unfolding drama.

"Why are you making such a scene?" It was Dorothy from the gamble tree window.

Henry exploded. Dorothy's absurd decision to come and live in this fashion wasn't just a slap in his face. It was an affront to the Empire, their Britishness, their heritage.

"The buggy's waiting Dorothy. Stop this nonsense and let's go." He grabbed at her hand as she tried to shut the window. "Come on."

Dorothy's face came down on his hand. She tried to bite herself free from her husband's vice grip. "I'm not going back. Your Khasi woman is pregnant." She hissed.

"So that rascal's put a spell on you. You slut! Mother of all whores! That's what you came for? To fornicate with that godman fellow?"

Munshi tugged at Henry's arm. Jatadhari rose from the riverbed, stark naked. Water dripped from his dreadlocks, running down his shoulders in little rivulets. He seemed to be emerging from some deep trance.

As he strode through the crowd, calling: "Ma ... Ma ... Chhinnamasta. Ma ... Ma Chhinnamasta! Ma Mahadevi. Ma Dhumawati, manifestation of Goddess Shakti who made herself, a widow. Ma ... Ma!"

Brown's eyes met the jatadhari's. He shivered. Something inside him seemed to crumble. He leaned heavily on Munshi Vepin as they stumbled back down the path.

Two brahmins had set up shop at the Hanuman Gate. They had brought rice from Coochbehar and sales were brisk. Two servants assisted them. A small crowd had gathered. It was difficult to find this quality of joha rice for sale in Kamrup. As the news spread, people from Natpara, Hemtola, Bamunpara, Bezpara homed in on the makeshift stall to buy this special rice.

There was sympathy in the crowd for the middle-aged brahmins in coarse dhuties and chadars. As young men, they had not been able to afford the bride price. So they went to Coochbehar, hoping to make a fortune performing religious rites. But time flies and now they were back. No brides. No money. Every now and then they would shout at a customer haggling over the price with their servants. Once in a while, the malnourished servants would add to the commotion.

A great many people were going up today. Devotees, wrapped in shawls and blankets. Dew falling from the leaves of the towering trees had soaked the huge rocks on the hill.

Today, this auspicious second night after the full moon, was the wedding anniversary of Shiva and Parvati. Kameshwar, the god of love, was taken around the temple on a silver palanquin, before the formal installation of the Lord in the temple. The women's voices rose in song:

O Goddess Rudrani, Devi Parvati, enticer of Shiva, your heart is as hard as the stone from which you are wrought.

Without warning, some twenty young men in dhuti kurta appeared. "Beware of the jatadhari. Women, beware! Get out Dorothy Brown! Go home!"

The louts rushed down the hill, pushing and shoving everybody in their path. Devotees from far-flung Coochbehar and North Shekhadari couldn't tell what was going on. They had no idea who Dorothy Brown was. They were climbing up chanting, "Ma ... Ma ... Tara. Ma Bhairavi, Ma ... Ma ... Ma."

Among them were Debeshwar Sarma and Harakanta Sarma, in Shantipuri dhuti and turbans. They were large landowners from the north bank. Their sons were students of Cotton College. Both the boys had disappeared from their hostel. Before John Simon set foot on Assamese soil, a government circular had been sent to their guardians, indicating that any student participating in the anti-Simon demonstration would be rusticated. The two brahmins had come to see if their sons were hiding among the conspirators at the Chhinnamasta temple. They saw the joha rice but paid little attention. Both carried stout sticks. Speculation was rife about a government plan to impose a ceiling on land holdings. Both prayed wistfully that their sons Shibanath and Ramgopal would one day become lawyers and let them breathe in peace. The path was overgrown with wild shrubs and creepers. They had to use their sticks to clear the way ahead. A drummer lay prostrate before a trident wielding ascetic sitting by a statue of Ganesha. On seeing them, the drummer got unsteadily to his feet. "Hai prabhu, I am Pulu, the drummer."

Harakanta Sarma was taken aback. "Aren't you from Borka ... or is it Mokhuli? Are you ill? Or is it opium?"

The drummer knelt at Harakanta Sarma's feet. "Prabhu, I have fallen on bad times. My elder son is very sick." He grabbed at Harakanta Sarma's feet, weeping.

Harakanta Sarma stepped back. "What are you doing?"

The drummer wiped his face with the gamocha on his shoulder. He said hoarsely: "He's got tuberculosis. We have been ostracized."

"Who has tuberculosis?"

"My son, Gajen."

"How?"

Debeshwar Sarma, who had been watching quietly, spoke up. "I saw him last year, during the Deodhwani." Pulu had come with the drummers from Kaihati, Dimow, Borka and Mohkhuli. Thirty drummers had accompanied the twenty one deodhas or dancers, representing different gods and goddesses during the annual festival. "Wasn't he Bogola's mount?"

Pulu was sobbing. He pressed the gamocha to his mouth. "Hai Prabhu, he travelled all over Assam, learning to master the drum. He even learned the tinipak ghurile and could make a triple turn as he played. He trained with a master in Coochbehar. Now he cannot leave his bed."

"I heard he even learnt how to make drums."

"Yes, he did. Dhalar Satra in Upper Assam taught him to sing. Remember? You clapped when you saw his performance."

The drummer continued, "My son! He would leap like a wolf, when he sang those songs."

Pulu began to sing. The tune fell somewhere between a dirge and a ditty. Harakanta Sarma kept his distance as he tried to comfort the drummer. "May Almighty Mother relieve you of all anxiety. Mahadevi! O Chhinnamasta! Ma ... O Ma!"

All three chorused: "Ma ... Ma ... Ma Devi! Ma Bhairavi, destroyer of all sorrow!"

Leaning on their sticks they took a few steps forward, then stopped abruptly. Debeshwar Sarma whispered to Harakanta Sarma: "Pulu could take us to their houses. Who knows, the fugitives may be hiding near the Kautilinga temple. The drummers go there to smoke ganja." Harakanta Sarma nodded.

Soon, Pulu was tagging along.

"Listen Pulu, take us by another route. We want to visit the drummers' quarters."

Pulu took the lead. But this short cut was covered with brambles. The two men were just not used to roughing it. They rested for a while on a huge boulder by the side of the road. They couldn't help but notice the drummer's skeletal appearance. They had never seen a man in such a state.

"You are in bad shape, Pulu!"

"Worries sir! Worries over land, worries about my son!"

"Where is your land?"

"It is on the Borhi side. The river has eaten up half of it. The other half is mortgaged. When I went to get it back, I was told ..."

"What?"

"I asked them to release a part of it. They shouted at me.

They said the land was not a sacrificial goat. The head couldn't be separated from its body."

They resumed their walk. The silence was broken by a clamour from the temple. It must be crowded inside. The pot-bellied priest was probably offering obeisance to Hara-Gauri.

With Pulu in tow, the two men explored every narrow, untrodden path. They peered into the mouths of caves hiding behind the thick foliage. They poked around in the undergrowth with their sticks. Ideal places to conceal a cache of arms. Exhausted, Debeshwar Sarma and Harakanta Sarma were acutely aware of their advancing years.

"We may as well stay on for a couple of days. We'll be able to make a more thorough search."

"Sir! What will happen to me? I could not carry on living if my son were to die. Please help me with some money to take my son to Gauhati for treatment."

Pulu fell at their feet. Again Debeshwar Sarma stepped back.

"Last week our priest told us about the foreign lady. It seems she brought out some ointment and bandages for our women's hands."

Harakanta Sarma nodded.

"Listen Pulu, go and lie on the veranda of Darbhanga House. I have heard that the foreign lady has a whole lot of silver coins stamped with the likenesses of King George and the Queen."

With this helpful advice, both gentlemen hurried off in search of their own priests.

"Ma ... Ma ... Ma Chhinnamasta! Ma!"

Dorothy Brown sat up with a start. It came from the direction of the Chhinnamasta temple. It was midnight. Jatadhari must be deep in meditation. Khat, khat, khat, khat. Aah, aah, aah. The clatter of buffalo hooves met the invocations of the jatadhari. What was that? An owl? A bird on a tree near the veranda? Hook, hook, hook. Sounds floating up from the Brahmaputra. The last gasps of a dying man. Why was the buffalo being dragged off for sacrifice in the middle of the night? What sort of worship is this? A man clanged a brass plate. Tong. Tong. Tong. Khat. Khat. Khat ...

Dorothy could see two mournful eyes shine at her through the night. She sat up. The click of retreating hooves kept time with her heartbeat. Khat, Khat, Khat. Could it see its way in this dark? The stone path – hard and cold as the hearts of the men pulling it. Khat. Khat. Khat.

When water is poured over its neck there will be a stampede. Ropes, pitchers of water and milling humanity. The men's groins grew hard. Erect as ramrods. As they dragged the buffalo to its fate. It doesn't want to go. It's frothing at the mouth. It empties its bowels.

"Ma ... Ma ... Ma Katyayani. Saviour. Keeper of us all ... Ma ..."

What sort of deliverance is this?

Dorothy's underarms were damp with perspiration despite the cold. The nightdress clung to her. She lifted the mosquito net and got out, turning up the lantern. A mosquito whined in her ear. No, she could not possibly open the window at this hour. The mighty Brahmaputra lay naked. Exposed.

She poured water from the pitcher into the silver glass, and took a long draught. Her hair slid to her shoulders like molten copper.

"Ma ... Ma ... Ma Chhinnamasta!"

There was nothing to fear. No need to hesitate. No dishonour. She opened the door and picked up a lantern. No eyes stalked her. Slowly, steadily she walked to the cave below the temple of Chhinnamasta. The door swung open as her foot touched the step. She could see the jatadhari at the altar. His skin gleamed bronze in the light of the oil lamps. The russet locks coiled like serpents down his bare back. His eyes glinted like the flames of earthen lamps that were lit in buffalo heads, sacrificed for the boon of a long life. Only a patch of red cloth covered his genitals. Hibiscus flowers lay strewn about, like fresh blood.

"I knew you would come."

She climbed down the stairs to him.

"No peace of mind?"

She did not reply.

"No one can claim peace of mind."

She turned her eyes from his face.

"We hold our souls together with the skins of sacrificed animals. No peace of mind." He reached for an earthen pot and took a swig of local brew as he rose. He signalled her to come closer. She sat on the lowest step hugging her knees. His raw odour wafted to her.

Picking up another earthen pitcher, he drained it. He lifted an earthen lamp from the altar to her face. Her copper hair gleamed like a machete.

The lamp light flowed down her sharp nose, the soft lips. It rippled down the smooth curve of her fair neck to her full breasts. A rush of waves. A gentle tremor. The silken spread of light engulfed them.

Ratnadhar waited on the banks of the Brahmaputra. He was all set to sketch portraits of people sailing over to this side. The river was quiet, flecked white, as though drizzled with ash from the sacred fires of the altars. The shadows over Bhasmachal had turned the island into a silent black rock in the heart of the river.

A large boat came in. Devotees from Kuruwa. Two sick people were helped off the boat. There were two young girls in the party, dressed in cotton mekhela-chadars with puff sleeved blouses. Two young men dragged a pair of goats roughly off the boat. The animals bleated in pain.

Faithful to the jatadhari's suggestion, Ratnadhar had busied himself with the portraits. His drawing materials were arranged neatly on a flat stone near the battle rock. Every now and again the wind lifted up a sheet of paper and flung it on the sands.

The jatadhari had sent Ratnadhar to the British encampment near the Kalipur hermitage to show his paintings to a highly appreciative British clientele. His themes, obviously influenced by the jatadhari, were intriguing. There was a painting of Emperor Aurangzeb, who had bestowed the river stretch known as the Jalmahal, on the people of the Brahmaputra. He was hated by many – for there were stories that he had used the stones from the temples he demolished at Mathura to weigh meat. But this painting showed him in a different light. The Brahmaputra shone like the diamond on the emperor's finger.

Another portrait had King Kameshwar Singha's second wife, Madhavi Devi sharing a palanquin with his favourite mistress Rupoti Khatoniyar. The palanquin was delicately wrought with silver motifs. The royal seal was on her finger. Golden pins adorned her hair. The women's necks and ears glittered with elaborate jewellery, etched in the honey-coloured sap of the jangphain tree.

The story went that the Chairing king stole the second queen's jewellery in 1852. The queen had lodged a formal complaint with Captain Holroyd, the principal assistant agent in Gauhati. Ratnadhar had even drawn a picture of Captain Holroyd arguing about it with Colonel Jenkins.

The paintings spurred the white men on and the camp resounded with long forgotten yarns. The talk veered round to King Purandar Singha who on March 2, 1833 bought his sovereignty from the British for an annual sum of fifty thousand rupees and an undertaking to do away with corporal punishment. There were also tales of how the king was given a nineteen gun salute on his investiture as a constitutional monarch. Inevitably Captain McMaran's name came up, and juicy anecdotes were recounted of the goings on in his tent while Gauhati was under siege. Eventually he died of cholera, the storyteller said. On his deathbed, he warned: Drink only boiled water. Boil or you'll broil.

And don't go near that temple. A den of black magic. Somebody there has put a hex on me.

Ratnadhar's blood ran cold at the thought of the Kamakhya temple. He never dared look up at it. But the temple bells would not stop clanging in his head. Ratnadhar stared at the white men. He had picked up a smattering of Sanskrit in the valley schools, the Sanskrit tols. He had been to Palasbari and Sualkuchi with his friends. But English?

The Britishers discussed Dorothy Brown as if he weren't present. Dhap. Dhap. Dhup. Dhup.

Ratnadhar felt the .303 bullets hit his chest. Whenever anyone mentioned Dorothy Brown, a pain stabbed at his heart.

The portly Britisher in shorts turned to his sandy-haired compatriot, "What's the latest on the Brown woman?"

The six footer in khakis said, "Made some bundobast with that sadhu fellow, so I'm told. Cheeky devil."

Another aimed his rifle at a grapefruit, "Not likely. She's moved, lock, stock and barrel into that Raja chappie's mansion."

A wave of dismay washed over his remark.

"Oh, I say! Tch ... tch ... tch ..."

"Gone native ..."

"More's the pity."

"She's ruining her life."

"Give me the money for my paintings," blurted Ratnadhar.

The white men pulled themselves together. Their pockets were filled with coins stamped with the likeness of the queen. The elaborately moustachioed clerks, who had brought the sahibs' tiffin boxes and water bottles, scurried up to load the paintings onto the waiting horse drawn carts.

Ratnadhar's heart was pounding. Dorothy Brown's name was

on the Britishers' lips. What were they up to? New faces had appeared at the Swargadwar and the Hanumandwar. He had noticed some suspicious characters climbing up the path from the bank. Would they harm her? He wasn't sure. Ratnadhar took a silent oath to protect this English woman with his life. Such soft eyes. Such beauty and grace. He was overcome with a wave of tenderness.

Ratnadhar gathered his things. But he wanted to stay under the huge gamble tree on the Amrajuli bank and watch the boats come in. Today he would count the boats one by one.

Bidhibala might come.

He had been counting boats for the past six months. She had promised to come at festival time. So many festivals had gone by. Durga Puja, Nabanna, Madan Chaturali, Rajeshwari Puja, the fast of Sath Deodhwani. Bidhibala had not returned. Her hair must have grown longer. Her braid would hiss like a poisonous snake when she bathed in the river. She would not be permitted to worship at the Chhinnamasta temple.

As Ratnadhar walked towards the water, memories of Bidhibala came flooding back. The first time he met her was at the Kumari Puja.

As she sat on the dais, Shambhu priest argued with a couple of devotees. "The girl seems to have crossed her twelfth birthday. Let's check her hands, feet and chest."

"She has breasts!"

"She must have reached puberty."

"It's just greed." The kumaris were offered gifts of saris, money, mirrors and sendur.

Hai – a heinous sin!

Pandemonium broke out. Bidhibala's father, Singhadatta Sarma, prostrated himself at the door and said, "If the girl has come of age, let Ma Chhinnamasta strike me with her machete. Let her strike me twice."

Yes, Bidhibala did look old for her years. There she sat, on a mat of kush grass. Her hair untied, touching the floor of the dais. Her feet were painted red with alta. A huge sendur bindi marked her forehead. Ratnadhar had come here with his father after taking some devotees from Tarabari or Kholabari around. It was not the veneration of one kumari but of several. There were various three and four-sided motifs on the floor. Two virgins from the lowest caste, two from the merchant caste and two from the brahmin caste. On those who were venerated before puberty, would be bestowed the fruits of worship of the entire pantheon of deities.

What had come over him when he saw Bidhibala? His father had had to drag him away from the place.

"Ratnadhar, some devotee has brought a buffalo. Apparently they've been performing this sacrifice for the last seven generations. Come away. Don't ... You cannot look. It will only upset you."

Ratnadhar could remember it all. A boat was approaching. A cloth curtain hung below the canopy.

But no. It did not come this way.

A small boat docked. Some ruffians jumped out. He could not recall having seen those faces before. They trooped up the jungle path behind the curly haired man with the pock marked face. Something covered with a large shawl was slung over his shoulder. A gun?

Ratnadhar followed them. As they neared Darbhanga House he broke into a run. He imagined they were Britishers in the guise of revolutionaries. Who knew? Nowadays anyone and everyone claimed to be volunteers and ate with the Malipara and Bezpara crowd. Whenever they heard a police whistle, they dived under the beds. Dorothy Brown's face floated before him as he scrambled up the path.

He could hear the jatadhari's voice in the distance.

Ma ... Ma ... Ma Chhinnamasta!

That evening, Ratnadhar's duty was to rally volunteers for the jatadhari's protest march. The curious gathered round. Even the children had come to watch the poisonous snakes come out of the river to crawl over the ascetic's body.

Ratnadhar had organized the rally in secret. His instructions from the jatadhari were to approach students in the Sanskrit tols. But Ratnadhar wanted to ensure a good crowd. So he had stood at the iron gates of Cotton College and under the sonaru tree on the banks of Dighalipukhuri. From the vantage points he could catch the Cotton College students on their way to class in Curzon Hall. He passed on the jatadhari's message. But the ones who had heard about Ratnadhar's madness on their earlier trips to Kamakhya avoided him.

Midnight. Tap tap tap ...

The jatadhari had hired a night watchman for Dorothy Brown.

Silence.

The guard slept on.

Another knock!

"Who's there?"

A muffled sob broke through the darkness. Should she open the window?

Tap tap tap ...

She put her ear to the door. Only the roaring of the Brahmaputra.

Dorothy cautiously unlatched the shutters and peered out. A strange man stood there, his hair like spiky thorns in the dim light. His eyes were two sunken pits.

"Who are you? What do you want?" She tried to sound calm.

"Aai. I am Pulu, the drummer. I am in trouble. Please help me."

Hesitantly she raised the lantern to take a closer look. The man was just skin and bones. His clothes were drenched. It must have rained. "It is still dark. Come back in the morning."

"If I come in the morning they will see me, Aai." The man protested

"Who will see you?"

She stood at the window. The moonlight filtering through the foliage glanced off the man's face. Strange. The shower seemed to have imbued the Kamakhya demigods with new life. The statues had been ravaged by the sword of Kalapahar. The raja of Coochbehar had invaded Kamarupa in the early sixteenth century to avenge the dishonour of his excommunication from the brahmin fold when he married the daughter of Badshah Suleiman Kararani of Bihar. Dorothy's nightgown and flowing hair complimented the moonlit forms of the scattered demigods.

"Come inside."

The guard woke up with a start as Pulu entered. "Aai, what are you doing?"

Dorothy raised her hand, "I have asked him in."

Cautiously the drummer entered and squatted in the far corner. His stench filled the room.

"What is the matter?"

"My only son. He has tuberculosis. I have to take him to the hospital in Gauhati today. I don't have any money. We are drummers. The river has eaten away all our land. We have nothing left."

"A drummer?"

"Yes."

Pulu lifted his hands. Dorothy had never in her most terrifying nightmares seen human hands quite so disfigured. Are those the hands that beat the drum? The gnarled veins stood out like dried and crusted intestines.

The guard standing on the veranda cut in, "Don't believe a word he says, Aai. It's the opium."

"Opium?"

"Why do you add to my troubles?" Pulu whined. "If I don't take him to the hospital today, he will surely die. He is vomiting blood."

Dorothy set down the lantern. She pulled a trunk out from under her bed.

The drummer stood up. In the light of the lantern he could see Dorothy take a cloth bag from the suitcase. The bag slipped as she fumbled to open it. Coins with the queen's seal spilled all over the floor. Raising the wick of the lantern, Dorothy said, "Pick up the coins. Take them."

The drummer fell to his knees, snatching at the coins. Without a word he rushed out of Darbhanga House and vanished into the night.

Unable to go back to sleep, Dorothy went over to the table. She took up a pen and composed a letter to her friend, William Smith, of the Steamer Company:

"I have two Promissory Notes that I want you to encash. I wish to make a will with regard to my property. Please help me."

She added a few more lines before she carefully sealed the envelope and placed it on the table. For a flickering instant she gazed at the lantern, her thoughts seeming to waver. Then with a sigh she picked it up and went to the door. Her steps quickened as she neared the temple of Chhinnamasta. The jatadhari was praying. Softly she went down the steps, her nightgown coming unbuttoned as she went. In the muted lamplight, the shadows criss-crossed her face. A hapless fish, ensnared in the boatman's net.

On the next full moon night, we shall present a memorandum to the priests." The jatadhari addressed the gathering. "Can we rally about two hundred people?"

"O Reverend One," the front row chorused, "There will be more than two hundred people. We have passed the word to all the schools. We have even informed the tols in the valley. A big group of students from Cotton College is also planning to join the procession. We just need to fix the date, time and the auspicious moment." The jatadhari raised his hands heavenwards, "Ma ... Ma ... Ma! Cast off your blood stained robes."

His disciples took up the refrain. "Ma! Ma! Cast off your blood stained robes. Adorn yourself in garments of flowers ..."

Just then a large crane fell from the sky at the jatadhari's feet. It had been hit by a stray bullet. The students shouted, "We *must* ask the white men to move their shooting range."

"It's the third time this has happened."

Gently, the jatadhari lifted the dying crane and cradled it to his chest. Then, raising it lifeless, to the sky, he murmured a prayer. A few students took the bird from him and went down towards the river. The jatadhari sat down again and was soon deep in meditation.

Plans were underway for the protest march. A memorandum against animal sacrifice was to be submitted to the head priest. But little headway had been made. They had hoped that the jatadhari would announce the date and time. But he sat in silent meditation. This was the first time he had slipped into a trance in the middle of a meeting.

A black and yellow serpent crept out from the leaf litter to coil itself around the ascetic's neck. "Snake!" shouted everyone, including Ratnadhar. The jatadhari continued his meditation. The devotees leaned in closer, signalling their warnings.

No one could tell exactly when it slithered out of the dreadlocks and down his back, to disappear into the undergrowth. As the bizarre scene played out, the jatadhari's eyes remained shut. By now the crowd of devotees had doubled.

A tall, thin student from Cotton College waited eagerly to have his say. It was almost an hour before the ascetic finally opened his eyes. "O Reverend One, the English woman's presence is causing much distress. Newcomers have been getting off the boats. They're prowling around the complex. The other day, in front of the Hanumandwar, I came face to face with a man carrying a revolver. Gandhi's volunteers, hiding in the jungles, are not at all pleased with the situation. Please ask her to go away before the demonstration."

"Ask her to leave," another student pleaded.

The jatadhari raised his hands and looked skywards. Then

he closed his eyes again. That instant, Dorothy who was sitting behind a bush, stood up and said firmly in Asomiya, "I have come here of my own free will. No one can ask me to leave." She turned on her heel and stalked off. In the stunned silence that followed, all eyes were on Dorothy's retreating back. Nobody had ever heard a white woman speak this way. They had occasionally seen this fire in the speeches of the Assamese women who had joined the movement for independence. Some in the back rows shouted, "Whatever she may say – surely the white men will take it out on us."

One of the student leaders muttered, "The police is all over the place. They are scouring the jungles, digging out skulls and gold bangles. It seems they belonged to some priest's wife who threw herself on her husband's funeral pyre."

A student who had come all the way from upper Assam to take part in the procession was puzzled. "Sati? On the banks of the Brahmaputra? Remember, King Kumar Bhaskarvarman's mistress? She threw herself on his pyre. But none of his wives committed sati. Or is that just some old yarn?"

Another remarked, "I have heard that the Brahmaputra looks terrifying from the rock where the woman committed sati. Do you know who she was?"

In the midst of this hubbub, the hermit from Torsa, skulking behind the shrubbery croaked ominously, "The curse of Chhinnamasta Devi will blast you to oblivion. Your endeavours will come to naught. The very plan you are hatching to stop animal sacrifice will turn on you like a sword of slaughter. Your blood will flow on the sacrificial altar."

"Human sacrifice has been banned a long time. We will adorn the goddess with beautiful flowers. We shall offer her our own blood if need be. But this must stop." The others joined in, "Yes. We will offer our own blood. We shall put an end to animal sacrifice."

The disciples whispered among themselves. Buffalo hooves clacked in the distance. Two tantriks in red joined the hermit from Torsa. "This sorry state of affairs in the country is all because human sacrifice has been prohibited. Evil spirits have taken charge of the land. Only he who is prepared to sacrifice his life to the goddess will be redeemed of his sins. Human blood is the nectar of the goddess. He who offers himself to her is lord of the universe."

The fat tantrik mumbled a shloka to the goddess, as if reading a message from an invisible draft. A tall dark figure with deep-set eyes standing next to the hermit from Torsa took over. "O faithful! Evil spirits prevail because gross infractions were committed in the rituals of the goddess. They have taken over this heaven on earth. O men of faith! I have been witness to a human sacrifice and I yearn to see the sight again.

"That glorious man was bedecked with karabi garlands, hibiscus and other fragrant flowers. His body was painted with white sandalwood. It glowed like the sun dried hide of a goat sacrificed at the altar of the goddess. He was bound in chains."

He held his audience spellbound. "The man on his way to the abode of the goddess instantly became a god. The rituals were performed strictly in keeping with the *Kalika Purana*. The one who offered the sacrifice wept in anguish. Falling at the man's feet he prayed to him. May your favours protect me from fiends, servants, kings and other ferocious wild animals."

Two men in the assembly cut in. Together they said, "That was the end. We know, we heard. They rushed in just as the blade was raised."

"Who came?"

The audience was all agog.

"The white men's soldiers. On white horses."

"Did the white men ride over the altar?"

"They fired rifles in the air."

"Did the worshippers run in panic?"

"What happened to the man with the sandalwood paste on his body?" An old hump-backed tantrik harangued. "Cursed are those who try to stop the offering of animals!"

The tantriks retorted in unison, "What curse? Do we not already bear the lash of the Britishers? Where are our rulers? Where did King Rudrasingha go? He, who sacrificed a thousand buffaloes on the eighth day of every fortnight? Where are the rulers who built temples to the goddess, who covered brick and mortar with gold leaf? Do you know what those scoundrels did with the man painted with sandalwood paste ... do you know what they did?"

A midget pulling on a funnel-shaped clay chillum pipe heckled the three tantriks, "Oh, so you want to bring back human sacrifice, do you?"

"Only the other day, the revenue collector from the north bank sacrificed three buffaloes. Did it do him any good? He died two days later."

"You will rot in hell!" roared the old tantrik.

"Have you seen the golden snake on the Goddess Manasa? A reward for the sacrifice of ten goats."

"Golden snake?"

"Yes. A golden snake."

"Didn't Subhabrata, the goldsmith from Dakhala, stand one full day and night before the goddess, with a lamp burning in the skull of a sacrificed buffalo? The *Kalika Purana* says that such men attain prestige and immortality."

The midget jeered, "Where is Subhabrata? Where is the immortal goldsmith?"

The congregation joined in, "Where is he?"

By then the crowd around the old tantrik had grown. A few youngsters from Malipara and some of the young men who hung around the Soubhagyakunda encircled the tantriks. The hunchback thundered, "You will all rot in hell! Even a king offers an animal to ensure victory!"

The trees shuddered. The jatadhari's eyes opened. "Ma ... Ma ... Ma!"

Immediately all eyes were on him. His chant was powerful, resonant. More powerful than the tantrik. "Ma ... Ma ... Chhinnamasta!"

The devotees who had come to join the protest march took up his refrain.

Trident in one hand and a garland of blood red hibiscus in the other the jatadhari strode towards the temple. The congregation trailed after him, mesmerized. The louts who had come with the sole intention of disrupting the procession froze, stones and sticks in their hands. Even the stray dogs and the goats let off by Muslim devotees, after they had been offered to the Goddess Manasa, followed the jatadhari.

I t was dawn. Dorothy Brown, clad in overcoat and boots, walked down to the Brahmaputra. At the sound of her boots a large tortoise splashed back into the river.

Something rustled in the bushes. In the distance, a pack of jackals slunk by.

Was someone following? God only knew. She had been warned often enough. "Such early hours are unsafe. There may be wild animals around."

Dorothy turned to look. No one. The clip of a horse's hooves came to her over the gurgling of the water. Native officers, wearing riding gear over hand woven dhutis and gamochas, were training to ride. It was more or less mandatory for government officials to ride. They started off very early in the morning.

Again, that rustling in the shrubbery.

"Who's there ..."

Silence.

The Brahmaputra's turbulence lay ahead. Gasping, like a castrated goat in the midst of the sacrifice. The dawn rising in the east, dyed the sky red like the goat's blood soaked pelt.

Dorothy stumbled up the slope, sure that she was being followed. Had Henry deputed someone? Or was it a khadi clad volunteer? But she was confident that no disciple of Gandhi would lay hands on a woman.

A large bird flapped noisily over her head. What bird was it?

The rustling once again.

"Who? Who?"

Breathing hard, she took a short cut back to her quarters. On the veranda she looked behind her. The hermit from Torsa was scuttling away. Dorothy washed her hands and face in the makeshift shed of Darbhanga House. Then she lit the kerosene stove on the table.

The watchman was up by now. He went off to wash up.

Dorothy made two cups of coffee covering one with a saucer for the watchman. After a while she came out. She was in for a surprise. William, in loose trousers and a felt hat, was getting off the boat. Ratnadhar, in dhuti and shirt, walked up ahead, showing him the way. Dorothy went forward to receive them.

They were both very pleased to see her.

Ratnadhar rushed around, dragging out broken chairs and cane stools.

William said with typical enthusiasm, "Received your letter ... well I never ... Dorothy – if this isn't the most weird and wonderful place ..." He walked down from the veranda looking around. "How marvellously exciting! But Dorothy, can one possibly live here?" Then he added, barely able to hide his curiosity, "There's so much talk about him. *I must meet him!*"

Dorothy was silent.

The well built, genial William pointed at Ratnadhar. "If I hadn't met this young man," he said, "I would have still been wandering all over this sacred hill searching for you."

Dorothy smiled. "You will always find him by the river. He's waiting for Bidhibala."

"Who's Bidhibala?"

"Bidhibala is Ratnadhar's friend. His family are their official priests. She lives in Sualkuchi. You've been to Sualkuchi, haven't you? I remember you told me how you were mesmerized by the golden muga silk threads. Not to mention the women there, with their glowing complexions that seem to be woven from silk."

Ratnadhar blushed, unable to hide his embarrassment.

Dorothy continued, relentless. "Ratnadhar is a talented artist. He was painting all of last week. Would you like to see his work?"

She lifted the cover off a canvas. William went to take a closer look. Dorothy explained eagerly, "The jatadhari, the ascetic from Chhinnamasta, suggested that Ratnadhar try painting some scenes from the history of Assam for posterity. Look at this – the Ahom King Rudrasingha who reigned from 1696 to 1714. He is about to set out on a campaign, and has come to pay obeisance to the goddess. He is at the Hanumandwar with his army of soldiers, the horses and elephants. Look at this. He is mounted on an elephant and has commanded his men to fire in the air to salute the goddess.

"He's done such a good job. The king's personality is so well portrayed. He has been painting right here. On this veranda ... do you know William how many soldiers the king raised, to succeed in his various campaigns with the blessings of Ma Kamakhya? Four hundred thousand! The day Rudrasingha came to Kamakhya, the sacrificial altar was washed away with the blood of countless buffaloes."

"Dorothy, I really would like to get to know him. I've heard he is educated and enlightened. I want to learn the history of this mysterious place. I want to know about his healing powers."

Dorothy remained silent. She knew who William was talking about. No, she did not want to discuss the jatadhari. William took the hint.

He sipped his coffee. "Dorothy, I have come prepared. Two men, Henry Creed and Arthur Brown have had their wills made in Gauhati. I have Arthur Brown's will with me. He had it executed by a brilliant Cotton College student, Umakanta. This should give you a fair idea. Umakanta specifically requested me not to divulge the details of Arthur's will, but I will read it to you anyway."

William extracted the paper from his bag and read aloud. She listened earnestly to a will executed by an Englishman on Indian soil:

"Umakanta – you may perhaps know that I am much concerned about the provision for my common law (Khasi) wife. She has been almost my only comfort in these weary years. But for her I could not possibly have stayed on all those years at Gauhati. I would have run the grave risk of finding myself in the padded room of a madhouse. I have bought her some land in Laban and built on it a largish mansion and two small houses. The two latter ones she will let out. There is also ground for vegetables. Of course she is well supplied with jewellery and clothes et cetera and will have all my furniture. This land is absolutely hers by Khasi custom, so you will not be concerned with it.

"I have also bought Government of India 3½ per cent Promissory Notes to the face value of Rs 15,400. These are at present with Grindlay's Bank, Calcutta in my name. The bank collects the interest every six months for a small commission and this they will continue to do. These notes, however, and also a sum of several hundred rupees is to pay my wife her allowance the first year (whilst the interest on the notes is being collected). Early November, I shall legally transfer these to a body of trustees by a Trust Deed registered at Gauhati. This will benefit my wife during her life, and to me or my estate at her death. Amongst these trustees, Professor Rowland Thomas will be the sole acting one. He will not have a good deal of trouble ... the bank will collect the money and remit Rs 40 to my wife every month by money order, there being left in their hands a fair sum for their expenses and commissions. But there will be some trouble for getting back from the Income Tax authorities the income tax, which will have been deducted at source, at the maximum amount.

"There would not be this trouble indeed if my wife had been a subject of British India, and not technically a subject of the native state of Mylliem. But for this fact the Income Tax authorities at Shillong would have granted her a certificate of Income Tax exemption, but as it is they haven't the jurisdiction unless they are able to assume that she is a subject of British India (which is at present doubtful).

"However this possible income tax bother is the only trouble the acting trustee will have and this will only really be troublesome on the first occasion, for the rest will be a matter of routine.

"My wife will undoubtedly take a Khasi husband (for that is the universal custom amongst her people), but there will be no prohibition of him in the trust deed, and so the trustees need not bother their heads. The idea is that she is to have Rs 40 a month for her life, whatever she does or does not.

"The income tax onus will be on Professor Rowland Thomas in the first place however. It is only if he dies, or is unable to act, that the trustees must choose another acting trustee. In fact the other trustees are for no other purpose than to appoint another sole acting trustee, in the event of Professor Thomas's death.

"They will include Khan Bahadur Maulavi Ikram Rasul, the Superintendent of Excise at Sylhet, Mr Harold, Henry Creed of the Survey of India (who has a house and a Khasi wife at Shillong), Mr Reginald Ashe the present Assistant Commissioner of Income Tax of Assam. Both Mr Ashe and Maulavi Ikram Rasul can advise as to how to deal with the income tax trouble (if any) ... The Maulavi has himself a large amount of 3½ per cent government papers and gets refunds of income tax every year. You will see I have made the trustees as strong as possible. But they are all fairly old or as is Mr Ashe's case not likely to be permanently in Assam. I should much like to add you to the list my dear Umakanta if you will kindly allow me do so ..."

William had copied down Arthur Brown's will in long hand. So he had no problem repeating its contents. William looked up at Dorothy and said, "Mr Brown had a house built for you at the Sukreshwar embankment in Gauhati, which is probably in your name. Anything else?"

"There is no other immovable property here but I have a few Promissory Notes."

"Those trees, all around the house, would fetch a good price, Dorothy. But who will be the beneficiary of your will?"

Dorothy was silent.

William asked a second time: "Tell me who will you name as your beneficiary?"

Dorothy said quietly, "It is for the Khasi woman's child by Henry Brown, who until the other day, was my husband."

"What!"

"You heard what I said!"

William was losing patience. He fumbled for words. "But unlike Henry Creed or Arthur Brown, he has not married the woman! You see, he still hasn't married this Khasi woman!"

"I shall still make the will even if the child is a bastard."

The sound woke Dorothy. It was the middle of the night.

Those drummers, again! Since Pulu's visit, drummers from Mohkhab, Borka, Dimou and all sorts of other places had been coming to Dorothy with hope, their ribs sticking out of their cages. Unable to pay up the fines imposed by white men, they were now selling off the last of their possessions, even kitchen utensils. The government was desperate. Money was needed to maintain the Assam Regiment, brought in by the British, to break the backbone of the Peacekeeping Volunteer Force.

"Break them, break their drums. If they can't pay the fine, take their pots and pans."

Dorothy sat up. Should she open the door? Could it be the Congress volunteers or the community service men from the temple?

It sounded as if someone was pelting the door with stones. Fumes from burning cloth rose from the street. Someone was probably making a bonfire of British made garments close by. Such were the times. People were eagerly responding to Gandhiji's call for non-cooperation – to boycott courts, government educational institutions, legislatures and foreign clothes. Dorothy's heart beat faster.

"Open the door!"

She was certain that the volunteers would not harm her. But, could this be a conspiracy? Could it be the Gurkha sepoys?

Dorothy called for the watchman. There was no one there.

The jatadhari had swum across to Bhasmachal early in the morning and had not returned.

The ancient door of Darbhanga House shook, as if struck by an earthquake. Lumps of plaster began to fall off the walls. The door crashed open.

Men rushed in. They were ransacking the room. Two ruffians pounced on her, ripping open her nightgown. Before Dorothy even knew it, her sensibilities were violated. Darbhanga House reverberated with echoes of pain. Then, with some miraculous burst of strength, Dorothy, spread eagled on the floor, brought one knee up hard into the groin of the man about to mount her.

When the police came, she was lying there, half naked, scrapings of human skin and blood under her fingernails.

Eight syllable mantras had been uttered over a clod of earth, which was crumbled and spread around the charity hospital in order to secure it against wild animals. A skinny lad accompanying the midget said, "I had also learned a mantra to tame tigers from the jatadhari. It has to be recited eight times over a lump of soil and then thrown away."

He whispered the incantation in his companion's ear, "Om Hring hring hring shreing hron hrong hing."

The midget said, "A student from Cotton College came to the jatadhari to learn the mantra to win the heart of a girl from Dakhala. The jatadhari refused to oblige. So he went to the tantrik from Gaur, even paid him some coins with the queen's seal. The tantrik taught him the Chamunda invocation from the Kama Ratna Tantra: *Om bhagawate rudraya chamundaya / nayantara me bashamanaya swava....*

The lad asked, "Who was Nayantara?"

"The girl from Dakhala ... but listen, the root of the kaurithutia creeper and seeds of three or four others must be ground together, mixed with semen and rolled into pellets. The girl must be fed the pellets after the Chamunda mantra is invoked over them one hundred and eight times. They say that even if the girl dies, she will go on weeping, even in the cremation ground."

"What?"

A loud guffaw from the young men. The midget was offended. "The mantras were from the Kama Ratna Tantra."

The boy added. "Dorothy must have been fed some such mantra!"

One of the jatadhari's disciples said impatiently, "Shut up you louts!"

Then he called, "Ma Chhinnamasta! Ma, discard your blood stained robes! Ma! Ma!"

Voices echoed in the distance, "Ma! Ma! Discard your blood stained robes ..."

Some students from Cotton College broke into an animated discussion.

"What is the woman eating these days? Is she getting a share of the sacrificed meat?"

"After all, she comes from a line of meat-eaters. Her race has conquered the world!"

A middle-aged hunchback pushed through the knot of people, "No, no. I went to deliver water upstairs. The watchman was serving the lady her dinner. She has turned completely vegetarian. Lives on fruits and vegetables. The jatadhari's watchman goes off regularly to look for fruit. The fruits in Assam have a special flavour – she eats Indian palms, ripe bakuls, jamuns and figs. Even ripe jackfruit. She won't touch fish or meat. Doesn't accept meat from the offerings. She even sent back a dish of Kharikajoha rice and mutton curry."

A buggy stopped under the banyan tree. The bells on the horses' necks were still jingling. Henry Brown leapt out. Students clustered around him. Clad in khaki shorts, Brown strode decisively off towards the hospital.

Under the tree a whisper arose, "Oh! the foreigner can't forget the woman."

"I just don't know ... can't understand ... how Ma Narasinghee, Ma Ugrachandi, Ma Sarvabhutadamini, Ma Balapramathini gave this young woman the strength of a full grown elephant!"

"I heard she gouged out a fistful of flesh from the cheek of one of her attackers. He will be easy to identify now. Ma Ugrachandi came to the white woman's rescue." The reference was to Shiva's consort, the eighteen-armed goddess in her fearsome manifestation. Everyone chanted, "Ma Ugrachandi! Ma Ugrachandi! Ma! Ma!"

Henry Brown pushed his way through the crowd of onlookers. Two foreigners from the Steamer Company joined him. They had been waiting under the tree all morning. They were identically dressed in shorts and felt hats.

A watchman with a baton came out and dispersed the noisy stragglers. It was time for Dorothy Brown to go to the police station to identify her attackers. Curious lookers-on thronged the police station. There were security guards all over the place.

Dorothy came out. She was in a skirt, her hair loose. Her hands were covered in bandages. She was escorted by William Smith and a few other gentlemen. They went straight to the buggy outside. Everyone saw Henry try to take her hand. But she ignored him. Lifting her skirt with a bandaged hand, she walked resolutely on.

The silence was audible. It was impossible to even imagine her being the target of such a violent attack. Dorothy glanced back at Ratnadhar who was following the white men. She signalled him to come forward. Hitching his dhuti up to his knee, Ratnadhar raced forward to stand beside her. Dorothy said softly, "Stay by my side, I'll be needing your help during the identification."

Henry glared at Ratnadhar.

Dorothy did not speak to anyone else. She climbed up into the buggy and sat with William. Ratnadhar got in with the driver. Henry had expected that Dorothy would go with him – but that did not happen.

The three buggies trotted towards the police station.

By then, those who had gathered at the police station for a better view had already been chased away. Only the absolutely incorrigible had, like monkeys, shinned up the banyan and the mango trees. Never before had a white woman come to a police station. The buggies came to a halt. William and Ratnadhar stepped down. Henry came running over to assist Dorothy. But she stepped back and took William's hand instead.

They entered a large spacious room inside the police station. A tattered servant pulled at the rope of a cloth fan hanging from the ceiling. Ratnadhar recognized the boy. He had worked as a water carrier for one of the priests. They passed through, to go into another room. As they reached the door, the guard at the gate directed William and Ratnadhar to wait outside. A foreigner from inside said aloud, "Only her husband may come in with her."

Someone from outside yelled back, "She doesn't live with her husband any longer!"

Henry Brown, who had been standing by the door, burst out, "Rubbish! We aren't separated."

To their collective astonishment, Dorothy Brown said, "We don't live together. My friends, William Smith and Ratnadhar will accompany me."

A voice from inside said. "Friends are not allowed."

"All right then, I shall come alone," Dorothy retorted. "I shall identify the culprits. I still have the skin of one of them in my fingernails. Where will he hide?"

Several uniformed officials sat in the inner room of the police station. Dorothy had met most of them before, at church. The busy official must be the police inspector. He flaunted a heavy moustache. The officers rose as she entered. They doffed their hats and squirreled them under their armpits. The inspector indicated a wooden chair and asked Dorothy to sit. It had been set very close to the door of another room.

The accused would probably be led out through this door. Dorothy stepped forward and sat down. An official offered everyone water.

The tall officer whom Dorothy had met in church asked, "Will you manage on your own, madam? Shouldn't you call Henry in, to assist you!"

Raising her hand, Dorothy replied, "I'll manage, thank you."

Dorothy Brown was aware that she was the only English woman ever to have sat in the Gauhati police station. She was the only woman who had ever dared challenge the might of the British Empire.

The boy pulling on the fan coughed. A bell rang. The police inspector once again walked up to Dorothy and said, "They'll come out one by one, stand there, and look up at you. Then they will leave the room. As soon as you recognize the man, stand up and say: "This is the culprit."

Dorothy could see several hazy faces. Would she be able to identify the man? The man whose gouged skin remained embedded in her nails ... how could he escape?

Though the moving fan made some breeze, the cord puller, intent on the happenings around him often forgot his job. He would resume only when someone looked up.

The bell rang again. They heard the tramping of the sepoys' boots. Everyone sat up. A policeman stood at the door. Almost immediately, a young boy rushed in. He had long hair. His eyes were red. He wore a dirty vest and a dhuti pulled up above his knees.

Dorothy looked at the boy, "No!" Her hands would definitely have touched his long hair when she fell down that fateful night. He stood there for a while, then left by the second door.

Almost immediately, a tall, emaciated man also clad in a torn vest and dirty dhuti entered. He had thinning hair; beady eyes, parrot-beak nose.

He broke down. "Mother, would I do such a thing? I had gone to fetch firewood to cook for the students in the tol!" He wailed loudly.

A couple of sepoys hustled him out. Disgusted, Dorothy said, "Why have you brought these innocent people here? Where is the culprit? I tore his cheek. I shall recognize him at once."

The next man was short. He was older than the others. His hair was cropped close to his skull. A round face with beetling eyebrows looked straight at Dorothy. He shouted, "This country is our mother and superior even to heaven. Janani janmabhumischa swargadapi gariyashi! Janani janmabhumischa. Aai, we work for our motherland ... Why have they brought us here, alleging that we laid hands on another mother?"

He walked towards the door without any assistance.

"This is absurd!" Dorothy turned to the moustachioed police inspector and shrieked, "Who are all these people?"

The police inspector said in a busy tone, "There are more!"

Dorothy hung her head in shame when the next man was brought in. It was Pulu. He looked at her and said between sobs, "Aai, I was walking around your room, hoping to get some more help. With your generosity my son's been kept alive for a month now."

Dorothy jumped up, hysterical. "Let him go. His son is dying. What is going on? It seems even the poor villagers must shell out their share to keep the daroga happy."

All those present squirmed in their seats.

The daroga shouted brusquely, "There are more!"

Dorothy shouted over the din, "Bring me *that* man whose cheek I scratched with my nails!" Although the cloth fan was moving, Dorothy was perspiring copiously. Her copper hair was plastered to her neck – like a beehive to a tree. She fished out a handkerchief and dabbed at her face.

One by one, Dorothy had to review a score of men. Stunned,

she stood up and marched from the room amid pandemonium. William and Ratnadhar were waiting outside. She was disgusted, trembling with rage. As she stepped out, British officials of various rank and cadre surrounded her.

The short, jovial, cigar-smoking Hopkins of the Steamer Company came up to Dorothy. "Your husband Henry is waiting to take you home. Shall I call him?"

Dorothy glared at him. Hopkins' mushroom-coloured face turned pale.

William ran his fingers through his hair. "What have you decided? Where will you go? Dorothy, we are here to help you!"

Dorothy looked towards Nilachal Hill. "I shall go back to Darbhanga House."

William was astounded. "Go back? Think again. The house has most likely not even been repaired."

Dorothy strode purposefully towards the buggy. Ratnadhar was already inside. Leaning on his extended hand she climbed in and sat down. William joined her.

He looked perturbed. "I shall arrange everything. Keep a rifle handy. I have a .465 bore double barrel H&H Royal rifle. My friend, Smith acquired Colonel Gregory's .240 bore Apex rifle after he was gored to death by a buffalo during a hunt. I have a rifle in Smith's house as well. From now on you must be armed."

Dorothy was not paying attention. She merely asked, "Do you know who was behind this horrible attack?"

"Who?"

"Henry."

"Your husband, Henry Brown?"

"Don't refer to him as my husband!" she hissed.

Dawn was just beginning to wipe away the darkness of the night. The outline of a huge steamboat loomed through the mantle of mist. The jatadhari waited on the embankment with Dorothy and some disciples.

It would not be wise for Dorothy to live here after the assault. Suspicious characters were lurking about the temple grounds. Students from the tol had seen the shining barrels of guns, cleverly hidden in the undergrowth. Like snakes.

The boat came in. The disciples started loading the bags. The jatadhari's luggage contained an odd assortment of ritual paraphernalia – a conch shell, powdered snail shells, honey, hibiscus and aparajita flowers as well as several roots.

The ascetic took in the gurgling Brahmaputra. He looked at the trees on Nilachal. A flock of bulbuls chirruped in a mango tree. A bat flew past, almost grazing his nose. He would leave for an undisclosed destination before daybreak.

Everyone assumed that he was off to rally public support for his mission to ban animal sacrifice. The jatadhari checked to see that Dorothy Brown was all right. Though the boat had a canopy, she sat unobtrusively at its helm, clutching her parasol. Some disciples were still busy setting down her luggage.

The jatadhari looked at Ratnadhar amidst the chirping bulbuls, the chattering monkeys and the first flickers of dawn in the eastern sky.

"The light radiating from a divine soul raises the spiritual perception of every being. The atoms of this divine soul mingle with every living creature. The light emanates from this soul to engulf the cosmos. Ma ... Ma ... Feel it. Touch it. All is the same, all are equal."

Ratnadhar was on the verge of tears. There was still a childlike innocence about him. He had grown so close to the jatadhari and Dorothy that he couldn't imagine being separated from them. But the jatadhari constantly reminded him, "Life is a passage of separation; a heartless journey of disunion. Be prepared. Don't ever forget death. Only then can you live."

He drew the young man to him. "Listen Ratnadhar. We will be staying for a while in Maligarh and Chakrashila, before travelling further up. We shall return before Deodhwani."

Dorothy held out her hand, "I have entrusted my will to William. Keep in touch with him and ask him to have it ready for my signature by the time I return. If necessary, I shall go down to the valley."

Then the jatadhari said two very important things: "The students from the tol will meet to finalize the plan. It would be appropriate to hold the meeting at the Bhairav crematorium in the west. If the western corner of this crematorium is dug up, the skulls of men sacrificed before the goddess will be unearthed. If you dig at the southern end, you will find stains of human blood.

"Go from house to house on the north and south banks of these forty devotees who bring offerings for sacrifice year after year. Meet their families. Take the students from the school at Chatrakar with you. Ask the householders, if they have found peace from having sacrificed another's life for the sake of their own?"

Ratnadhar said eagerly, "Prabhu, I remember many things. Haladhar struck not once but twice trying to behead the sacrificial animal. The merchant from Shekhadari. He sent five buffaloes for sacrifice because he was suffering from tuberculosis. He didn't live six months. Who killed Haladhar? Hai Prabhu, I shall tell you of many things. Yesterday I had a dream, the Mother Goddess whispered in my ear. The fragrance of flowers from her body touched my nostrils. The scent of kharikajara, togor, bakul and lemon flowers ..."

The jatadhari looked intently at Ratnadhar. "Start painting. Spend more time at the crematorium. Tell everyone that we shall return before Deodhwani." He handed Ratnadhar a pouch with money and continued, "The doors of Dorothy's room are broken – I hope you remember. I have instructed the carpenters from Goroimari to repair them. Don't brood Ratnadhar, sit on the veranda of Darbhanga House and work on your portraits. Listen, you have to make two more portraits besides the Mother's. The old head priest Gangaprasad would make a good subject, fleeing with the Ahom King, carrying the Mother's statue during the Burmese invasion. Try to bring out the condition of the temple in 1817. Remember, the Burmese became followers of the Mother Goddess ... and remember also, that though the head priest had removed the statue, the Burmese did not ransack the temple. Feel it deeply, before you begin to paint. Mingimaha, who commanded the Burmese invasion, ruled Assam for about three years. During that time, he raised the contribution made by the Ahom Kings for Durga Puja at the temple. The Burmese, who roamed every corner of Nilachal however, never set foot inside the temple. Show the entire temple complex swamped in blood when Rudrasingha visited the temple."

A brace of ducks dove into the river, then bobbed up to the surface. Lifting his arms to the sky, the jatadhari called out again, "Ma ... Ma!" in the semidarkness his skin gleamed like newly burnished copper. His sinewy frame mesmerized Ratnadhar.

"When will you be back? I shall paint the temple flooded with blood. You will see it on your return."

The jatadhari gave Ratnadhar his blessing. "I shall return in time for Deodhwani," he said as he boarded the boat.

Ratnadhar stood there until the sound had faded. From the helm, Dorothy watched the men receding on the bank.

It had been raining since morning.
It had rained all week.

The temple doors were shut. The Mother Goddess was menstruating. Her loins were covered with a red cloth. Every year, on the seventh day of the month of Ashaad, the temple closed for three days. It reopened on the fourth day.

The stone steps were slippery. The rain had washed the blood off the altar.

The officiating priests were digging up the devotees' old records. The leaves of these ancient books were tinged red. The names of devotees from Puri, Nadia, Dinajpur, Srirampur, Nepal, Benaras and even distant Uttarkashi were recorded on them. Their pages were coming loose. It was that time of year when Ratnadhar's father sent pieces of red cloth to devotees who had availed of his services the previous year. He fished out the record books, and placed them on the table with an inkpot and pen.

Ratnadhar had been a great help last year. But this year he was busy with other things. Manomohan wrote down a few addresses. He got up to walk towards the Soubhagya Kunda. A few priests were already sitting on the tank's stone steps. He joined them. Utsav purohit said accusingly, "You seem to have handed Ratnadhar over to the Jatadhari from Chhinnamasta!"

"How long do you think the jatadhari will stay on in this peeth!" retorted Manomohan. "Haven't you noticed that everybody's fed up? When all is said and done, it was he who helped Ratnadhar. If I stop my son from associating with the jatadhari now and he gets worse – what then? Remember how the drummer Chandi's son had a complete breakdown when he saw a goat being sacrificed! He was taken to the north bank for treatment. He stayed there with a family for a month. They put him in a pit for three or four days as part of the treatment. He died on the fifth day."

"What need had he to watch if he couldn't bear it?" The priest in red demanded.

Manomohan continued, "Anyway, Ratnadhar has been totally cured by the jatadhari's prayers. Now he is completely immersed in his painting. How can I interfere?"

His logic silenced them. Shambhu purohit quickly changed the subject, "Such a terrible experience ... and still that white woman wants to come back. We all knew she was under the jatadhari's spell from the very first day. He must have used the Chamunda and Biswabashu on her."

"Chamunda and Biswabashu?"

"Yes, the only mantras with the power to bind so inextricably. Now he has sailed off to muster support for his crusade. The man will rot in hell. It is only a matter of time before he falls at the shrine of the eternal Jagadamba."

Who can say, what will happen. It is the white man's rule. Our days as officiating brahmins are over. We were appointed guardians of the temple by the Ahom kings themselves. But the white men dissolved the office. They managed to collect enough signatures to make it happen. How long do you think will it take them to get them moving?"

Another priest chimed in, "The stores, the treasury, everything functioned smoothly when the brahmins were in charge. We all know who got the upper hand after the system was abolished. Anyway, Manomohan, we just wanted to tell you something. Your son ... people have seen him lurking around the shed where the goats for sacrifice are tied. A couple of days ago, someone released a buffalo. A devotee from Upper Assam had brought it. Parameshwar Purohit presided over the rituals."

One of the priests sitting around retorted, "The buffalo was found near the Janardarn temple."

A water bearer arrived in time to add, "The devotee didn't want to offer the buffalo since it had been freed."

"Good. It was a suckling calf."

Haladhar purohit thundered, "Scoundrels! You will burn for your impertinence. The sacred texts very clearly state that the blood of a deer satiates the almighty goddess for eight months. The blood of a black bull or a boar appeases her for twelve years."

The finger of suspicion seemed to point directly to Ratnadhar. The priests and their hangers-on were apprehensive. A ban on animal sacrifice would deprive them of their ration of meat. Manomohan stood up.

In the kitchen, his wife Bishnupriya and Deba, the girl from the north bank, were chopping vegetables. All her life Bishnupriya had been cooking for her husband's patrons. Her skin was chapped and black from constant contact and exposure to the heat of the kitchen fires.

Manomohan pulled up a low cane stool and sat next to Bishnupriya. "What do we do about Ratnadhar?"

"Why? He seems fine. The screaming fits have stopped. Remember how he wouldn't let any of us come near him when things got really bad."

"People suspect that he is the one who's been untying the animals brought in for sacrifice."

"Oh Durga! Ma Chhinnamasta!"

Bishnupriya and the maid folded their palms, turned towards the temple and bowed.

"What do we do? The jatadhari has gone off with the white woman to rally public support. There were so many new faces at the goddess' sacred quarters during Ambubachi. Ratnadhar must be collecting their signatures."

"What signatures?"

Bishnupriya turned pale.

"Stop animal sacrifice. Ban animal sacrifice. That's what they sign." Deba spoke up. "Human sacrifice stopped only after it was legally suppressed in 1835. How long would it be before the Britishers banned animal sacrifice as well? Who in the world could stand up to their power? Their taxes had sent so many into bankruptcy – but had anyone raised a voice in protest? Even Gandhi was said to be calling for a ban on animal sacrifice at the Dakshineswar temple."

"Oh no! Ma Chhinnamasta will curse my son."

Bishnupriya broke down. Deba was moved to put a consoling arm around her. But she held back.

It was forbidden for Bishnupriya, the daughter of a high caste priest, to touch her. If their hands brushed even accidentally, Bishnupriya would have to bathe. Manomohan walked up to his wife and said, "Why are you crying? The boy is all right now. Isn't that all that matters?"

He remembered something he had to tell them. "You're going to have your hands full soon. I met Parasu Purohit near the Kautilinga temple. His wife just gave birth to a son. So he asked me to stand in for him until the purification rituals are done. Some pilgrims from Sualkuchi are expected. They want to offer a buffalo. Rich people!"

Their faces brightened. Deba exclaimed, "I shall ask for a muga silk mekhela chadar. But if they don't give me one, I'll make do with a red saree."

Manomohan asked Deba, "Do you know who's coming? When I went to fetch water for Parasu purohit I heard some talk that Bidhibala was expected."

"Bidhibala?"

"Don't you remember Bidhibala? The Kumari Puja ... the big fuss?"

"What happened?" Bishnupriya asked.

Deba glanced at Manomohan then whispered to Bishnupriya, "They suspected she had already come of age. Her father laid his head on the sacrificial altar and swore that she had not. That was the only way to save her. Her skin is like fresh milk. And her hair ..."

"Her hair?"

"Hazari Barua saw her hair and was smitten."

"Why is she coming here?"

"I hear her marriage has been arranged. The groom is from the north bank. Owns four or five granaries. Plus two wives.

He's well past his prime. Must be over forty. Oh! The girl is like a mermaid!

"Someone started a rumour – that she had already begun to menstruate. So they were frantically looking around for a groom. Some brahmins who had come back from Coochbehar came forward."

There was commotion outside. Three servants arrived at Manomohan's doorstep carrying the luggage. Two slender young men came with them. Each had a centre parting in his thick hair. They were both very light-skinned, and dressed in Shantipuri dhutis and coloured shirts.

They helped an old woman up the stairs. Her mekhela was tied at her chest. She had wrapped herself in a chadar, its flowery motif woven in muga silk in an old fashion. Like other aristocratic brahmin women, she wore only unstitched clothing. There was no gold galpata, round her neck. No keru in her ears, nor bangles on her wrists. She was a widow. Behind them, came Bidhibala, treading carefully up the steps. Her mekhela-chadar was of pat silk. The long braid touched the floor. A servant boy followed behind them with a little buffalo, coming to a halt when he reached the stairs.

Manomohan seated his guests and hurried out. "Go, tie up the buffalo by the tank," he said to the lad. Today quite a few buffaloes have been brought to the tank. You must learn to recognize this one by its horns." The lad dragged the buffalo away. Its hooves echoed into the distance.

Tomorrow, the doors would be thrown open. This year, the Ambubachi had attracted a rush of ascetics and hermits. People from distant places were still pouring in. The faithful touched the earth with their foreheads, murmuring into the swelling tide of shlokas. Manobhaba, the Mother Goddess was enshrined within the cave in the form of a red stone. Touching the stone granted freedom from the cycle of rebirth.

Most of the crowd joined the long queues passing through the eastern door. The belief was that entry from the east side guaranteed wealth. More people poured in through the northern and southern doors, ensuring their own salvation and the acquisition of property. Nobody entered through the western door if they could help it. It was the portal of doom. Even then, one or two tantriks not only walked through the western entrance, but set up meetings with their patrons there. The rush of pilgrims at the Ambubachi was indescribable.

Devotees had come from all over. From Bankura, Dinajpur, Rajsahi, Nadia, Uttarkashi, Benaras, Gaya, Bindhya, the Tarai region of the Himalayas. Some had arrived by boat. Others had walked the distance. Some were fearful in appearance. Their matted locks, dusty as the hills, spreading out like many pythons. Some wore just the koupin loincloth. Some had painted their bodies with ash. Three Vaisnavites with flowing hair carried their tridents through the northern door to join the assembly by the side of the Soubhagya Kunda. They had been making the sacred Kamakhya pilgrimage for years now. Since the temple doors were closed for Ambubachi, a huge crowd swarmed around the Soubhagya Kunda. The water in the tank was murky. The Raja of Darbhanga had built a separate tank for the goddess. Even this water had taken on a coppery hue. The devotees were all around the temple. Every now and again, the Vaisnavites' voices rose over the clamour. Ma ... Ma!

The Chhinnamasta courtyard was also packed. The jatadhari was in great demand. A student from the tol clambered onto a rock, "The jatadhari will come back." He told the devotees, "Ma Chhinnamasta has commanded him to return. The mother will no longer wear bloodstained garments. Deck her with flowers. Cover her in garlands of kathal champa, lotus, kanak, kaminikanchan, karabi."

"Ma Chhinnamasta, cast off your bloodstained robes." The devotees chorused, "Ma, adorn yourself in flowers."

The hermits danced around the temple, brandishing their tridents. "Cast off your bloodstained garments, Ma. Cast off ... Ma ..."

The police arrested a group of tantriks who were eating out of human skulls. More skulls were found in their cloth bags.

Ratnadhar had almost finished collecting his signatures. He was with a group of students from the tol. He knew his father would be annoyed. The small squares of red cloth would have to be sent to the devotees from Gaur, Coochbehar and wherever else, just before Ambubachi, as soon as the temple doors were opened. They would turn the cloth into amulets that would bring fulfilment of their desires. In the past, it had made Manomohan so happy to have his son by his side, helping him address envelopes. But now Ratnadhar had no time. The signatures had already filled up the pages of the books.

Ratnadhar, accompanied by the students from the tol, moved their campaign to the Koutilinga temples. They located the ascetics sheltering in the caves to escape the wrath of the white men's sepoys. Ratnadhar peered into a cave where these ascetics who ate from human skulls were hiding. They lay there, stoned on ganja. Ratnadhar was not inclined to approach them.

"Forget it," a student advised. "They'd only put their thumb impressions on it anyway."

A little further, they came across a crowd at one of the dilapidated temples of Koutilinga. Most of the worshippers were from Gaur. Some among them had gone to bathe in the Brahmaputra.

Two women draped in red-bordered sarees were cooking. They had conch shell bangles on their wrists. They had just had a bath in the Brahmaputra. Drips of water wriggled down their hair. A young girl not yet in her teens, sat some distance away. Her long tresses grazed the ground. There was a red sendur bindi on her forehead. Her feet were painted with alta and a garland of flowers was around her neck.

Ratnadhar called from the doorstep, "Where have you come from?"

The women bent over their pots. They exchanged a glance but did not bother with a reply. A student from the tol pulled Ratnadhar aside and whispered, "Don't you know? They are prostitutes!"

"Prostitutes?"

"Yes, they are prostitutes. They have brought the little girl to offer Kumari Puja. The most exquisite form of the goddess is the beautiful virgin Tripura. The scriptures say that those who offer puja to a prostitute's daughter will be greatly benefited."

Ratnadhar could smell the fragrance of gulacha flowers and jabakusum oil. A middle-aged woman came out and asked, "What do you want?"

One of the students stepped forward, "We have come with a special request."

"What?"

"There will be no more bloodshed on the Mother's premises. Those who want to see an end to animal sacrifice must put their signatures in this book."

"Are you trying to change the ancient rituals of the Mother? Sacrifice is deliverance."

The student from the tol explained, "The scriptures offer alternatives to sacrifice. We can also please the Mother with honey, milk and yogurt. It doesn't say anywhere that the rituals cannot be performed without blood."

"O Ma Durge, O Ma Durge! We cannot change what has been practiced for thousands of years. The Mother's womb must be filled with blood."

"Ma Mahadevi! Oh Ma Kamakhya kamrupinee."

The women in the river were shouting. The pretty girl in the red-bordered saree stood up to see what was going on.

Ratnadhar and the students went towards the river. In the distance they could see the lean muscular figure of Shambhu Sikdar, who's job was to behead the animals for sacrifice. His skin was the colour of copper. He was playing a bizarre game. There was a pile of grapefruit near the rock. He threw them into the river one at a time. As soon as the fruit bobbed up, he sliced it up with his machete.

Ratnadhar and the two students knew that once in the past, Shambhu had had to make three strikes to behead a buffalo. Since then he always practised his strokes on grapefruit at the same time as the white men's daily shooting practice.

Ratnadhar carried his inkpot and pen in a small bag tied to his waist. It was an odd looking bag, covered in ink blots. Standing at Shambhu's side, they were acutely aware of how futile it would be to ask for his signature. A frail student asked, "Perfecting your strike, are you?"

Shambhu grunted.

"Would you want your son to do the same work?"

Shambhu said gravely, "No, he's going to study. I'm going to send him to Varanasi."

"How many buffaloes have you slaughtered?"

Shambhu did not reply.

Ratnadhar cut in, "I know! My father said that you have beheaded two thousand buffaloes."

"Two thousand and thirty," Shambhudev corrected.

"Ugh ..." The three couldn't hide their disgust.

The short student plucked up his courage. "Would you mind very much if animal sacrifice were banned?" He asked.

Shambhu flung another grapefruit into the river. As soon as it bobbed up he expertly sliced it in half. He looked up at the boys, "I honestly wouldn't mind at all."

They stared at him, transfixed. But no one dared ask for his signature. Bewildered, they turned tail and ran, not stopping until they reached the temple of Chhinnamasta. They were awaiting the arrival of the jatadhari. All wretchedly poor, in tatters and bare feet. Drenched in sweat and rain. Should they ask for signatures?

There was talk that Ma Chhinnamasta had manifested herself in the white woman, Dorothy. She had acquired the strength of a wild elephant. She had after all ripped off a piece of her attacker.

Stalls had been set up in the temple courtyard. All sorts of items were on sale. Conch shells, beads, rudraksha garlands, copper vessels, stone and silver ware, pictures of Bengali dancers, portraits of foreigners, oleographs of Durga, Lakshmi, Saraswati; Shantipuri dhutis, Murshidabad silk sarees, marble figurines of Vishnu, and idols of the goddess cast in an alloy of eight metals.

Ratnadhar and the students took the short cut up the slippery steps. They would continue after lunch. Water dripped off the huge bhatghila leaves. Ratnadhar said goodbye to his friends and climbed up the stairs. He stepped into the guestroom. The inkpot and the pen slipped from his hand. He was face to face with Bidhibala.

Manomohan's family rose well before dawn. Today the temple doors would open. People had been waiting in long queues all night. The line was quickly acquiring the character of Hanuman's tail. It had been a while since the temple's official cleaner, the aathparia, had entered. Oddly enough, he needed no lamp. The Mother's own radiance suffused the interiors.

The aathparia never spoke about it. Ever.

The water bearers carrying in the copper pots had had similar experiences. But they too never breathed a word. With some license, the faithful read meaning in their gestures. That was how the secret had come out.

On the eve of the great day – the third night – a few curious devotees tried peering over the temple walls to catch a glimpse of the divine glow. The water bearer, filling up his pots, noticed the bobbing shadows. "You will suffer the fate of Kendukalai. You will all be turned to stone!" He shouted.

Most of them had heard the story of the divine Ma's appearance before the brahmin priest Kendukalai, to dance to the hymns he sang. Kendukalai had demonstrated the divine Ma's dance steps to the great Koch King Naranarayana and was turned into stone. Strange, that this staunch devotee of the goddess would risk his soul for a glimpse of her dancing naked.

The furious goddess is said to have cursed him. "Hear me O King. If you ever dare raise your eyes towards my serene abode, your dynasty will perish. You will rot in hell."

Addressing the huddling shadows glued to the temple door, the water bearer shouted again, "You will be burnt to ashes. You will lie there like lumps of stone."

The midget who had hurt his foot limped up. "Wolves! You will be cursed. There won't be any bones left for your last rites. Get lost!"

The aathpariya emerged from cleaning up and decorating the temple. The priest, in fresh red robes, walked down the steps to the Soubhagya Kunda and then came back. At the door of the temple, he took a look around. By then, preparations were on, to make offerings in four, five or eight parts. Assorted odours of burning incense, camphor and fragrant flowers wafted from the temple. From the distance came the auspicious drumbeats and the chiming of bells. The women broke into a high-pitched wail.

As the third round of worship ended, drums were beaten. A crowd of worshippers milled around the sacrificial altar. There was a near stampede as they pushed forward to take a look at the plump, black goat. Its bleating sounded over the din. The past three days of rain had washed the altar clean.

There! A single stroke of the machete. A spurt of red. A group of devotees smeared their foreheads with hot blood. The tantrik with the mountain of matted locks, lay on the ground to daub his forehead with it. People saw him lick the blood. A dog ran in to join him.

The crowd closed in on the writhing headless animal. The pockmarked tantrik in red robes, stood on a mound of earth near the altar. "This is the first sacrifice in three days. The Mother is thirsty. Come, paint your foreheads with this blood. Listen to me. Stab the man from Chhinnamasta who tries to rob the Mother of her share of blood. Who will volunteer to stab him! Speak up!"

The devotees, with blood smeared foreheads, chorused, "We will stab him. We will."

The tantrik's voice rose over the hubbub, "Deliverance comes only when sacrifice is offered. Sacrifice alone will lead you to heaven. Mark my words. A buffalo's blood quenches the goddess's thirst for one hundred years. And when a follower offers the blood of his own body, she is satisfied for one thousand years."

"One thousand years?"

The tantrik invited them up, "Come forward. Come forward."

No one came forward.

Again the hideous tantrik called, "Come!"

A little old woman with a mekhela around her chest pushed through the crowd and threw herself on the floor by the sacrificial altar. Preparations for the offerings – with the head of the sacrificed animal – were about to begin. The woman cried, "A little while ago it was eating grass and leaves. Why did you kill the helpless soul? It was alive. See, see how it voided its bowels in fear. O you blood thirsty goddess, take my head as well."

She laid her head down on the altar. Her clothes were dripping blood. Chaos reigned. "Get her off the altar."

Two worshippers pulled her off. The tantrik, gnashed his

teeth. "Come forward. The scriptures say that all you need are two drops of blood on a lotus petal. Just two drops from your own body. Come, come. Anyone, who offers a bit of flesh, the size of a sesame seed, from his chest will have all his desires fulfilled within six months. A tiny scrap of flesh from the chest."

No one moved.

As if from nowhere, the temple midget appeared. "You cowards! You drag helpless beings to the sacrificial altar by rubbing chillies in their eyes. Then you behead them. Now when it comes to offering your own blood, you run away!"

No sooner was the goat's head carried away, than the worshippers dispersed. The goddess was clean again, after four long days. The faithful now scrambled for scraps of the red garment.

It wasn't long before the prayers wound up. Devotees who had queued up all night, entered the temple through the open door. Bidhibala's grandmother, her brother, Rudra, and his friend, Dambarudhar went in with Manomohan. They were carrying earthen lamps, flowers and garlands. But Bidhibala didn't come. She would be present on the day of the buffalo sacrifice. She had carried a crippling burden since the day that uncouth man had come to see her. He had blurted, "Oh how beautiful you are. Like an angel."

"A respectable landowner from Bangara. Has a wife and two daughters. No son. That's why he wants to marry again. Very rich. He will keep our daughter in comfort."

Her mother had retorted, "The man's hair and beard are already turning grey. Even those brahmins from Coochbehar were better."

"Shut up!"

Her mother could speak no more.

Bidhibala's father shot back, "Those wretched brahmins! Went to Coochbehar to scrape up the money for the bride price. What would they feed our daughter?"

Their discord sat heavy on Bidhibala's heart. From that day, she had almost stopped looking anybody in the face. She did not go to the temple with Manomohan. It would be some time before the special private worship for which they had come. They would be here for about another week. Draped in a red-bordered saree, Bidhibala was with Ratnadhar's mother in the kitchen, helping her cut vegetables. Her long hair snaked down her back. Though she had not as yet come of age, she seemed to possess a wisdom beyond her years. Her father had brought a buffalo on the boat. It was to be sacrificed. The thought distressed her. Earlier, she used to be thrilled to come on a pilgrimage to Kamakhya. She desperately wanted to meet Dorothy Brown and the jatadhari from Chhinnamasta. Two of her friends who had seen Dorothy had said, "You can't look straight into her eyes. Sometimes they dazzle – like pools of water lit up by earthen lamps. Sometimes, they glow like embers smouldering on the hearth."

Acrid smoke filled the kitchen. Bidhibala retreated, coughing. "Bidhi, sit on the steps and cut the vegetables," Bishnupriya handed the girl the basket and the low wooden pira stool.

Ratnadhar was addressing envelopes. His table was heaped with them. Bidhibala was directly in his line of vision. He couldn't stop himself from looking up at her. She could feel his intense gaze glancing off her. Instinctively she straightened her clothes. Bishnupriya rose to introduce her son. "That is my son Ratnadhar. He saw you the last time at the Kumari Puja."

"Yes, I remember. He was at the amphitheatre," she said.

Bishnupriya went back into the house. As she turned, she said,

"Bidhi, you can call him Dada. He is six or seven years older than you." A smile danced on Bidhibala's lips. Ratnadhar beamed back at her. From inside, Bishnupriya said, "Ratnadhar, show Bidhibala the Darbhanga House when you are through. She was asking me all sorts of questions about the white woman yesterday. She wants to see where she lived. Show her the house and bring her back before the others return from the temple."

Bishnupriya's heart went out to Bidhibala. The very thought of this lovely young girl being married off to an old man was disturbing. But nothing could be done about it now. These things happened. A forty year old man would marry a child of eleven.

Ratnadhar picked up his clothes and went to the bathing area, partitioned off by a cane screen. He was dressed in a moment. No one noticed the tornado that swept through his heart. For the first time, something stirred inside him. An emotion long dormant had awoken.

He came up to his mother, "Let her come then."

"You can call her Bidhi. Deba will go with you. Don't be late."

Deba and Bidhibala were all set for the outing. In an instant Bidhibala hitched up her red bordered saree. They took the short cut which went through the neighbourhood of the serving priests. As they passed the wooden houses, young and old came out onto the verandas to catch a glimpse of them. A few even asked Ratnadhar, "Where is she from?"

Without an upward glance he replied, "Sualkuchi."

"Which family?" another asked.

Ratnadhar hurried to avoid the questions. Bidhibala and the maid trotted along, trying to keep pace with him. When they reached the Darbhanga House, they found the carpenters from

Goroimari busy with repairs. They had already fitted a new door to Dorothy's room. Her clothes and other belongings were locked up in the next room. Ratnadhar had the keys. He took the ring from his pocket and unlocked the door.

Bidhibala spoke up for the first time since they left the house, "When will she be back?"

Ratnadhar looked her straight in the eye, "She will come! The jatadhari's followers will come pouring in, to put their signatures to his petition. He has disciples everywhere."

"I know. I heard that when the boat capsized in Sualkuchi, during Shivratri, he saved two boys from drowning. They say that even at the height of the monsoon, the man from Chhinnamasta swims easily across the Brahmaputra. But what is he doing with that foreign lady ..."

A secret smile lit Ratnadhar's face. Here was Bidhibala right in front of him! He breathed in the perfume of her hair. Could it be true? The achal of her saree brushed against him. Was he dreaming? The river coursed ahead of them. She seemed to merge with the Brahmaputra's flow.

She stood on the veranda. The Brahmaputra raged past in a fury of churning waves and froth. Chunks of black wood floated by, like the scabs of old wounds from the riverbed, or the huge dome of some dilapidated temple.

Suddenly, Bidhibala dropped her shyness, "Is this the room where Dorothy Brown was molested? Everyone in Sualkuchi was talking about it." Ratnadhar was taken aback. He had not expected such candour.

"Yes. The doors had weakened with age. See, this one's new. It's made of teak. That's the old one, like the carcass of a dead cow." A scent clung to the room. It was the scent of Dorothy – a fragrance of lemon flowers mixed with the Brahmaputra waters.

Ratnadhar's painting gear lay in a corner. Some of the canvases had covers over them. Bidhibala wandered around the room for a while, trailing her fingers along the walls – as though over Dorothy Brown's face. She looked out at the Brahmaputra. The swell of rolling waves carried along lengths of wood and bamboo, like pallets of the dead.

Should he tell her? She shouldn't be marrying an old man with a wife. Should he confess his feelings for her? Clouds gathered in the sky, like smoke billowing from a hearth. Faint drumbeats pounded in the distance. Bidhibala asked Ratnadhar to take the covers off his paintings.

"The paint isn't dry yet. If you still want to have a look, go ahead."

Behind the covers, a group of men in blood red robes stood beside the Saubhagya Kunda. Ratnadhar explained, "These are the young priests and the old, the acolytes and the celebrants. That's the one who performs the sacrifices. In the background you can see the blood soaked altar."

Bidhibala knelt to take a closer look.

"Acolytes and the celebrants ... red dhutis, yellow pigment, layered hair, jewellery ...!"

"I can imagine what you want to know. Who inspired these scenes? The jatadhari taught me all this. He drew sketches in my scrapbook. He even specified what colours I should use. If you like I can show them to you." Ratnadhar was excited. "Look, another unfinished painting."

Bidhibala was almost thrown off her feet. The painting was of King Rudrasingha in death. A poignant depiction of the devotee of Ma Bhairavi and Ma Kamakhya, laid out on a boat. At his feet, was a follower of the goddess. At the helm of the boat lay the dancing girls, covered in blood, crushed to death between bamboo poles. In their hands were gold caskets, inlaid with stone. Gold waistbands were wrapped around their slim waists and earrings dangled from their ears. Blood, everywhere. The boat was being readied for its journey to the capital. In the background lay the lifeless heads of buffaloes offered to the goddess. Not one, but several.

Bidhibala found it all too disturbing. "What kind of painting is this?"

"The king had died in Rudreshwar. This painting shows what happened when the dead king's body was taken to the capital," Ratnadhar explained. The dead girls were suspected to be spies who had cast a spell on the King. They were sentenced to be crushed to death between bamboo poles. They say the girls were really followers of the goddess, and danced at her temple."

Oh! Bidhibala and the maid studied the picture. The sight of all that blood on the girls was terrifying. The paint was now quite dry, making the spilled blood seem real. Ratnadhar's powerful strokes articulated the pain on their faces. Such a ghastly death! Bidhibala shivered.

"How could they kill the girls when they weren't even sure?"

A tremor ran through Ratnadhar's heart. What difference was there between sacrificial animals and women? He wanted to warn her. Don't go to the altar Bidhibala. Tell them this wedding can't ... will not take place.

"Now show us the last painting."

Ratnadhar's reaction was sharp. "No. It will be too much for you."

Bidhibala was adamant. "I must see it."

"You won't like it."

"It must be the portrait of the English woman. A portrait of Dorothy Brown. I want to touch it. To feel her."

Deba warned, "What are you up to? It is time for your brother to come back. Let's go now."

Bidhibala pushed back against the wall and slid slowly to the floor. Deba called, "Get up Bidhi! Don't you hear the temple bells? Stand up!"

It seemed as if she had known Ratnadhar for a long time. He had no intention of showing the picture to anyone else. Some extraordinary power seemed to have possessed him to paint it. He had worked in a frenzy. Tears had rolled down his cheeks. His nails had turned into sharp weapons.

Even his father had expressed disapproval. "How will these paintings help you? Start performing the religious rites. Go to our devotees from Sualkuchi, Jagara and Dhuhi. Carry the offerings of the Mother Goddess and come back with money and clothes."

His mother had protested. "Let him do what he wants. He isn't money minded like the others." And turning to Ratnadhar, she had added, "But my child, you must not draw such things."

What should he do now? She was sitting there stubbornly. Suddenly he got up and threw aside the cover. Everybody stared at the painting. Buffalo sacrifice. Six or seven men were pulling at the ropes. The collar around its neck had split. The animal was desperately trying to break free. It was emptying its bowels. The terrified eyes. Pitchers of water splashed on its neck. Tremors wracked its body.

"It wants to live! Oh Ma let it live ..." Bidhibala moaned in pain before she went plummeting down the stairs.

Bidhibala was jolted out of her sleep. The little buffalo was lowing softly. She lay next to her grandmother. The old woman was snoring. Her grey hair laced the pillow. For a moment Bidhibala was dazed. Where was she? She saw the ten-armed goddess on the wall. In the hazy lamplight, she could almost feel the goddess' fury, threatening to break out of the frame. A large garland of marigolds adorned the picture. It must have been put there by her grandmother.

It all came back to Bidhibala. Someone had carried her from the Darbhanga House and laid her on the large bed.

Her thoughts wandered as she heard the buffalo again. Somebody had brought him from the tank and tied him in the shed at the back. It must have rained during the night. Her heart was in turmoil. It was just a baby. Bidhibala's father had bought the mother buffalo when her younger brother was ill. They had even sold the milk. Her little brother had not survived.

The doctors had failed to diagnose tuberculosis.

The calf bellowed again. It still needed its mother's warmth. Only because of her. Because her marriage had been fixed ... her heart pounded. She prayed to the goddess to take her life and spare the animal. Its cry was desperate. What must it be thinking? Should she go and check? Suddenly she could see the predatory face of the grey haired man to whom she would soon be married. He had shared the same bed with another woman for ten years. She would not say ... there were many things she wanted to say. She was wracked by thoughts of rebellion. That man! The very thought of him made her shudder.

Bidhibala got off the bed. She tiptoed to the door and slid back the latch.

She went out to stand at the wooden balustrade of the back veranda. In the dim light of the moon, she could see the buffalo below. She could hear the deer in the jungle. She could hear the coughing of the hermits gathered for Ambubachi. She could hear the sobbing of the drunken tantriks.

For all the sounds, a deep silence reigned.

Bidhibala quietly opened the door and went to the shed. She stood beside the buffalo. It looked up at her with huge luminous eyes. She had seen the calf grow up before her eyes. Its horns were not properly formed yet. When her father bought its mother, he had carefully checked its horns. A flawed horn was unacceptable. She had taken a sacred vow. She had stood for one full day and one whole night before the goddess, an oil lamp lit in the skull of a sacrificed buffalo in her hand. Her brother had died anyway.

There was nothing that his devoted father would not do. Now, he was sending this calf to its death. She could still remember how it had lost its way in the village one day and bellowed helplessly as it tried to find its way home.

In the next few days, it would be sacrificed. For her. Its head would be hacked off. For her.

She put her hand on the buffalo's rain soaked back. She wiped it down with her achal. The animal trembled. It was still gazing at her. What had come over her? Tears rolled down her cheeks. She sat down on the veranda steps. Should she run away? Just as Dorothy Brown had run away from her people to take refuge with the jatadhari?

She put her head on her knees and wept. The buffalo stopped crying. The Brahmaputra roared. The pale moonlight had bleached the river's heart to the colour of a faded rag. Without warning a large owl hooted in the mango tree nearby and swooped down over Bidhibala's head. The lamplight spilled over her long tresses, imbuing them with the lustre of snakeskin.

Just then the front door opened. Ratnadhar stood there, lamp in hand.

"Eh, eh ... what are you doing here ...?"

She did not reply.

"Are you ill? Bidhibala?"

She looked up.

"I am upset!"

"Upset? Why?"

He came to stand by her side.

"I want to tell you something."

"You want to tell me something?"

"Yes."

They went slowly down the steps and stood under a dimaru tree.

"Listen carefully. People say, you are the one who secretly releases the animals brought for sacrifice. Please let this buffalo go so I won't have to watch it being sacrificed. I haven't slept for nights at the thought. I've seen it grow up, seen its grey tufts turn black. When I bring his food and call "Mena," he runs up to me. I can show you now."

Ratnadhar quickly said, "No, no please ... I believe you."

"When I pass by him, he lifts his head to look at me." Agitated, she grabbed Ratnadhar's hand and pulled him to the buffalo. "Look, look."

The animal was gazing at her! It snorted, blowing two drops of water from its nose. Bidhibala looked so forlorn. She reached forward and held on to Ratnadhar's feet.

"I know that you are with Chhinnamasta Jatadhari. You have to help me."

Ratnadhar stepped back bewildered. "Aren't you afraid?"

"No."

"Haven't you read the scriptures? I've heard that you can read Sanskrit."

"No, I have not. Scriptures that prescribe such acts don't interest me. I know Sanskrit is the language of the gods, but I don't want to read such books."

"Bidhibala!" Ratnadhar exclaimed, "Always revere Ma Chhinnamasta. The *Kalika Purana* recommends tying up the buffalo or the goat's head in three ways. It says we must offer the best portion of the sacrifice to the goddess. It speaks, for instance, of offering the blood of a buffalo to Bhairav on the fourteenth day of Shuklapakhsa, the first fortnight of the full moon. But it also states that the goddess herself recommends offerings of white gourd, melon, sugarcane and alcohol. Nowhere is it written that one cannot worship without spilling blood."

"Really?"

"Look up the twenty fifth incantation of the sixty seventh chapter of the *Kalika Purana*. The white gourd, melon, sugar cane and alcohol are as dear to the goddess as goat's blood."

Dumbstruck, she watched Ratnadhar. A vein throbbed on her forehead. She suddenly seemed to gain new strength. Looking at him she said, "Even if you ask me a million times, I shall not read these scriptures! I have no use for scriptures that recommend the killing of animals."

Ratnadhar was perturbed, "Bidhibala!"

"Ratnadhar, I shall offer my songs to the goddess. Songs created from my tearful, unspoken words. I shall smash the stones weighing down my heart and offer their dust to the goddess along with flowers."

Bidhibala could hear her grandmother coughing. She stepped back onto the stairs. There would be a lot of talk if anyone saw them together in the middle of the night.

"Listen Ratnadhar, I shall come here again tomorrow night."

They could hear the jackals howling in the crematorium. The night birds called. The tantriks chanted their invocations. They heard the clanging of chains – in which the two hermits were bound – intermittently breaking into the silence.

The wick of the earthen lamp in Ratnadhar's hand flickered. What was she saying? That she would not read books that had anything to do with the spilling of blood?

The grandmother's coughing bout settled into silence. Bidhibala went back to the buffalo. It raised its ears and stared at her. As a baby, it used to run when she pulled its tail. And grandma would shout indignantly, Hey you! What are you doing?

"He understands everything! When I see those dark eyes in the light of the earthen lamps, I feel it wants to say something. Just like the tortoise in the sacred Bhairavi tank that crawls out when we call it Mohan, he used to look up when I called, even while he was suckling."

She burst into tears. Ratnadhar didn't know what to do. He looked up at the sky and saw a falling star. A night bird grazed his head, and flew off hooting loudly. In the distance he could hear a devotee call, Ma! Ma!

Should he touch her hair and comfort her? He could save the buffalo by taking it down the short cut. Should he tell her? Should he tell her what he wanted to say? Would he ever again find such an opportunity?

He could feel a stirring in his loins. His hands slid down below his waist, to the pleats of his dhuti.

Once again, the grandmother began to cough. Bidhibala got up to leave. Before entering her room she whispered, "Same time tomorrow night. I cannot sleep."

Students from the Sanskrit tols of both Upper and Lower Assam, from Dayaram Shastri, Banghshiram Sarma, Brindaban Keot and Cotton College had gathered at the crematorium to discuss ways and means to stop the practice of animal sacrifice. After the meeting they all stood under the spreading tree on the riverbank, waiting for the jatadhari's boat to arrive. So many people were roaming around in the guise of volunteers. On land, in the water ... What if the police detectives followed them to their hideout! Who knew what would happen?

The country was ruled by the mighty British, on whose Empire the sun never set. There were many stories about the Late Empress Victoria doing the rounds. There were claims that the empress was immortal. She was born every morning and died each night. She was a little girl at dawn, a young woman at noon, and middle-aged by the evening. She disappeared in the darkness of night, implying death, before she was reborn the next morning.

Britain had conquered the world. It was capable of anything! The blood sacrifices in the goddess' sacred abode would surely stop when the jatadhari and his supporters stood before the district magistrate of Kamrup and showed him the signatures.

They usually assembled under this jamun tree after their meetings. Today was no different. Ripe fruit stained the ground under it. The purple blotches looked like the bloodstains on the sacrificial altar. The boys usually tried not to step on the stains. Oars splashed in the water. Immediately all chatter stopped and the students came to attention.

Boats carrying merchants and pilgrims sailed in from various places. On the shore there was bedlam. As the boat touched the bank, the noises of the animals and the howls of the women from Gaur brought an almost festive atmosphere to the bank.

The students from the tols and the college waited for a long time. The mighty Brahmaputra roared its way forward. It had poured the last two nights. So much so, it seemed the rain could wash away a whole palace, an entire country.

A couple of boats appeared on the horizon, like ruins floating up from the riverbed. The whole place smelled of freshly butchered meat. This was the scent of the Brahmaputra. A student from Cotton College said, "A boat is scheduled to come in this evening. It may bring some news."

Meanwhile, a group of devotees with their foreheads smeared with blood and vermilion came and sat on the stones below the tree, waiting for the boats. They hid small squares torn from the goddess' red garment in the deepest recesses of their clothing. They carried water in small ghotis, bronze-necked pots, cloth bundles and garlands in their hands. Dambarudhar, Bidhibala's brother's classmate came with Ratnadhar. Dambaru was a Shandilya brahmin. His ancestors had been disciples of Damodardev, who propagated Vaisnavism. Their religion demanded supreme surrender to Vishnu who in the form of Narayana assumes the incarnation of his guru Srimanta Sankardeva from age to age. Though they were also devotees of the goddess, they staunchly opposed animal sacrifice. But every year their relatives brought animals to the altar.

Dressed in coarse dhutis and loose shirts, Ratnadhar and Dambarudhar stood with the other devotees under the tree. Ratnadhar carried the signature books in a bag slung over his shoulder. He went up to each one with folded palms and said over and over again, "You must be aware of our signature campaign. Please put your valuable signature on our book. Once we have the signatures, the white men will help us." He brought out the inkpot and pen from his bag.

His suggestion made some of those squatting on the bank uncomfortable. Their foreheads were red with vermilion and sacrificial blood. Although some seemed to waver two young men who were near the luggage got up. Ratnadhar held the inkpot, as they took the pen from him and signed the petition, unconcerned by their companions' frowns of disapproval. Others touched their hearts, as if to reassure themselves that their talisman from the goddess was secure. The priest's words still rang in their ears, "Listen to my words – your desires will be fulfilled if you wear the piece of red cloth from the garment of the goddess."

A covered boat was moored on the bank. All eyes were on the party about to board. They were singing to the beating drums and clinking their cymbals. Most of the group was made up of young girls. Two effete, longhaired men were playing the double-sided drum, the mridangam with them. Their eyes were lined with kohl, there were garlands round their necks, and they wore anklets. Ratnadhar guessed they were prostitutes from Rajashahi or Bankura. They had come for the Ambubachi fair. Two young girls in bright printed sarees, foreheads splattered with sendur and goat's blood, scampered ahead. They must have been brought for the Kumari Puja.

Dambarudhar watched them intently, pushing and shoving at each other. In the tussle, one of the girls fell into the river. In a flash, the mridangam player had dropped his drum and dived in, pulling her to safety. The other women surrounded the drenched girl, shrilly rearranging her clothes.

In the confusion, the fragrance of jabakusum hair oil combined with the sharp scent of perspiration wafted up to Ratnadhar and Dambarudhar. Before they got on, the musicians produced two bags, embroidered with motifs of swans and lotuses and delicately shook out their contents.

"Dambaru, do you know what's in those bags?" Ratnadhar asked. Not just Dambarudhar, but the whole congregation watched, fascinated by their antics.

"Come on, tell me why they shook out their bags."

"The bags contained dust from the prostitutes' doorstep. Besides the other essential offerings for Durga Puja, the five sacred articles from the cow, rain water, dew drops, water from a conch shell, water from eight pitchers, water from the hoof print of an ox, water from a golden pot, dust from a prostitute's doorstep is also required."

"Dust from a prostitute's gate!" Dambarudhar exclaimed.

"Young girls from the brothels, who have not reached

puberty, also take on the mantle of the Almighty Mother during Kumari Puja."

Ratnadhar turned to check if Pulu was around. But he was nowhere in sight. He could see only the drummers from the Mohkhuli and Boroka areas. Ratnadhar walked ahead, his head lowered. He had heard that Pulu's son had died. Since then, Pulu seemed to spend all his time smoking ganja, falling down in a stupor any and everywhere.

Bidhibala's face tormented Ratnadhar. Her tears seemed to have seeped into his heart. New shoots were bursting from the earth after the rains. Wild creepers tumbled from the urium and sotiana trees, almost entangling Ratnadhar and Dambarudhar. They were headed towards the Dhumawati temple, also known as the temple of Koteshwari. Dambarudhar had wanted to see some of the temples. He had jotted down the names in his small notebook. His father had told him to visit the Dhumawati temple. He had also asked him to see the idols that had been buried in the ground after the carnage let loose by Kalapahar.

"But did Kalapahar actually come to Kamakhya?"

"He did indeed!" Ratnadhar exclaimed. Who else could have hacked off the idols' hands and feet? The Burmese came in 1817. They hung around the temple but never touched anything. Instead, they raised the priests' honorarium. And the Mughal Emperor Aurangzeb? Hadn't he bequeathed one section of the Brahmaputra to the temple priests so they could collect water tax in honour of the goddess? Captain Welsh's huge army had also held back from damaging the temple. It was said that not even one tree had been felled. So who vandalized the temple of the goddess?"

"Is there any proper evidence?" Dambaru asked.

Ratnadhar replied, "Yes, there is. The white men recorded the events. It was more than five hundred years ago. The brahmin Kalapahar who had converted to Islam was commander in the Bengal ruler, Suleiman's army. He routed King Naranarayan's commander, and chased him to Kamakhya. He wanted to gobble up the entire land. There are so many stories! Folklore seems to have a greater power than history."

"Folklore appeals to the people," Dambaru said. "Ratnadhar, yesterday we saw a powerful performance of Kalapahar's begum. It was a local show. This story of the begum has never been documented by any historian. But yesterday's performance made her immortal."

"Where is that boy from?" Ratnadhar asked.

"From Gaur it seems."

"Gaur?"

"He spoke Bangla, though everyone could understand him. He threw in a couple of Persian words as well."

They walked on. The sky was overcast. The area around the Dhumawati temple was wild and overgrown. A group of monkeys chattered in a tree. The young men entered the forecourt. "Look Dambaru, this is where the raja of Darbhanga built the wooden staircase to the temple." He went on, "I believe it is quite acceptable that the courts appoint the temple priests. But I find it strange that the priests keep running to the sub-judge about these wooden stairs. There was a great deal of controversy over the staircase that the king used to go to the temple. The Darbhanga King used to look down from the top of this staircase."

"What did he look at?" Dambaru asked.

Ratnadhar had a good head on his shoulders. For all his problems he carried himself with a dignity far beyond his years.

He leaned over and whispered something in his companion's ears. Dambaru's eyes widened in disbelief. His eyes combed the temple compound. He looked for the stretch of the Brahmaputra that looked like a dappled white deer. He found the huge trees festooned with flowering creepers. Was this the rushing stream by which the Darbhanga King met the priest's fair young daughter? He could not share his throne with anyone but his wife! Ratnadhar had also told him who brought the beautiful young woman to the court as the king's wife. It was folklore, inscribed in blood on the pages of history! Dambaru didn't want to scrap the pages of history. No one wants to.

The legal dispute over these wooden steps ... The story of Annapurna Devi's temple ... The question of work share and rights on the property ... The transfer of the case in 1842, from the purview of British officials to a civil court. Dambaru wanted to know everything. His grandfather had mentioned some of these stories.

Dambaru had also read in the newspaper about the case challenging the chief priest's authority. He still remembered the views of the judicial commissioner. No one could inherit the title of priest at the holy shrine of Kamakhya. The head priest appointed priests through the process of selection. The British Government refrained from interfering in the religious rites and contributions to the temple. Officials prevented corruption during selection. There was no differentiation between the chief priests where the benefits of Dharmottar, donated land and water tax were concerned. The chief priests watched the ritual food offering to the goddess with hawk eyes, the bhog of madhuparka – a mixture of butter, honey, milk, yogurt, sugar, and donations – to ensure that nothing was amiss.

Dambaru distinctly remembered the one man who had challenged the directives of the judicial commissioner: "In the absence of men, women should be given this responsibility as they are better equipped for these jobs."

But the courts quashed all appeals on behalf of women. It was here that the Mother Goddess resided in every household. And it was here that the aspirations were scotched. Breaking out of his reverie, Dambaru asked Ratnadhar, "I have heard a lot about this jatadhari. Is it true that he has magical powers? They say the restless magpie settles down before him, to sing its melodies. The shy swallows are said to grow boisterous in his presence."

Ratnadhar nodded. Dambaru continued:

"One of his disciples said that he can stand on water. Is that true? Poisonous snakes are entwined in his matted locks."

Ratnadhar nodded again.

"They say he stays under water for hours. Is that so?"

Ratnadhar nodded yet again. Dambaru was a fair, well-built young man who wore his hair parted in the middle. He was curious, just like all the others.

"What do you think will happen if Dorothy Brown comes back pregnant? According to her husband Henry, she went abroad for treatment when she couldn't conceive. She was desperate to have a baby."

Ratnadhar looked intently at Dambaru's face, then turned away. He stared at the temple door as if he was trying to look past it, through to the inner sanctum. He was not unaware of the happenings there. Once, he had caught a flash of Dorothy's bare arm in the flicker of lamplight. They were the colour of the ivory figures in Bishnu Kinkar Goswami's almirah. What if something happened?

He broke into a cold sweat.

Ratnadhar walked up determinedly. Dambarudhar followed him. They stood for a while under the ancient peepal tree. Some spent bullets lay scattered beneath it. Dambaru picked one up. The shell smelled of gunpowder. Ratnadhar smelt the acrid scent of gunpowder. It reeked of death. The all-pervading smell of death assaulted Dambaru's senses over and over again.

No, no. He must not think about Dorothy Brown now. There were many more important issues on hand. This was a turning point. They sat on a rock at the top of Bhuvaneshwari. A few red clouds scarred an otherwise colourless sky, like open wounds.

Ratnadhar asked Dambaru outright. "Are you alright with Bidhibala's marriage?"

Dambaru looked at him quizzically. He was silent for a while. Then he said:

"My marriage was arranged exactly two years ago. Gifts were sent to the girl's family and the wedding was finalized. Otherwise I would have married Bidhibala despite the questions about her maturity. Now I have even brought the buffalo for sacrifice. I am not happy. No, I am not happy."

Ratnadhar grabbed Dambaru's hand. He was shaking.

"Ratnadhar! What is the matter?"

Ratnadhar squeezed tighter.

"What is the matter, Ratnadhar?"

"Dambaru! Dambaru! Please ... You must help me. Promise that you will help me."

Eyes open wide, Dambaru asked, "Help? How?"

The Ambubachi was over. Devotees were streaming back to their homes. Those who stayed on in the deserted buildings and the caves around Bhuvaneshwari noticed two tantriks meditating in the Brahmaputra waters. They were there all night, snakes entwined in their hair.

A couple of British officers who had turned up for shooting practice happened to see the tantriks' bobbing heads. They thought they would have some fun. They fired into the air to scare them out of their trance. But the tantriks didn't budge. So deeply were they meditating that it seemed as though even a bullet through the heart could not disturb them.

Ratnadhar and the students were off to Darbhanga House. They piled the signature books on Dorothy Brown's study table. Ratnadhar sat down with a Cotton College student to check that the names and addresses were in line with the thumb impressions.

Countless names and addresses. Signatures in Bengali, Hindi and even English. Two students went off to meet a munshi of the court to work out how these signatures would be presented.

Meanwhile, William had sent Ratnadhar a letter through Munshi Vipin Chandra. He had apparently discussed the matter with a sub-judge. Things were beginning to move. Ratnadhar had also received a letter from the jatadhari. He would be back just before Deodhwani. Dorothy wrote in flawless Asomiya, "My heart is sad for I have not seen you for so long. It is time to prepare yourself. May the goddess help you."

As if they were valuable ornaments, Ratnadhar carefully stacked the signature books in a trunk and locked it.

It was not yet dawn. There was pandemonium in Manomohan's house. The sacrificial buffalo had gone missing! Bidhibala's father, a tall, strapping man, had just arrived from Sualkuchi. Shrieking in alarm, he ran to the Soubhagya Kunda, asking everyone along the way if they had seen the buffalo. He even asked some of the local urchins to look for the buffalo down in the valley offering them incentives of money. He himself rushed down to Malipara, the southeastern part of the temple. All this running around made him breathless. He wasn't a young man anymore.

By the time he came back, Rudra, Dambaru and even Manomohan had gone off in search of the buffalo. Others sat in the courtyard, dazed. When he returned without the animal, Bidhibala's grandmother began to weep. "What will happen to the girl now? The astrologer saw the signs of misfortune in her horoscope. He predicted that this was an inauspicious time. How could a tethered buffalo run away?"

"Someone's played a nasty trick," Singhadatta Sarma roared.

"A buffalo has disappeared. I, Singhadatta will bring ten more buffaloes for the ten-armed mother. I shall wash her feet with blood for Bidhibala's sake." Huddled in a corner of the veranda, Bidhibala shuddered. She knew her father. He was capable of anything.

Her grandmother stopped weeping. "And how do you propose to find the money for the ten buffaloes? By selling your fields. Your son will have to give up his studies. Put aside your pride and face up to reality. Offer your possessions to the goddess. But don't go after the land that will one day be your son's."

"Quiet Aai! The buffalo disappeared from right under your nose."

He had had a different name as a baby. His father began to call him Singhadatta only when his temperament began to show. Singhadatta had in a fit of rage, once cut off his wife's hair because her accounts were not in order. People still talked about the incident. When he lost his temper, his family either stayed out of sight or kept silent.

Dambaru and Rudra came into the courtyard wiping the perspiration from their faces with their gamochas. They had scoured the riverbank. Neither the pilgrims nor the priests had seen a boat come in. The buffalo seemed to have melted into the darkness of the night. Dambaru and Rudra had even asked the white men who came to the Kalipur ashram for their shooting practice. But they had found no success. One man claimed that he had heard the splashing of oars late in the night. But he couldn't tell whether it was a tiger or a buffalo that had been ferried away. Curious onlookers from various neighbourhoods across the temple complex crowded into the courtyard of Manomohan Sarma's house. They had all heard about the calf's disappearance.

Zealous followers of the Mother Goddess exclaimed, "One by one, more than twenty animals intended for sacrifice have disappeared. We know exactly who the culprit is." There were dark threats of dire consequences.

In the kitchen, Bishnupriya's heart was thudding, her ears alert. She was quite sure that this was Ratnadhar's handiwork. It was a sin to put one's own flock in such a situation! But there was no way out.

Ratnadhar was stuffing envelopes with scraps of red cloth. He paid no attention to the commotion outside. Someone from the crowd yelled, "Where is Ratnadhar? Drag him out. He can tell us where the buffalo is."

This was not the first time that Singhadatta Sarma had heard about Ratnadhar's activities. On his last visit, during Bidhibala's Kumari Puja, he had been told about the campaign to wipe out animal sacrifice. But he had not anticipated being a guest at Ratnadhar's house. Breathing hard, his massive shoulders hunched forward, huge fists clenched, he barrelled into the clamouring rabble. "Shut up all of you," he bellowed, his face dark with malice. "Shut up."

The corrugated asbestos sheets rattled on the roof of the wooden house.

For the past month, Singhadatta Sarma had sat on a cane stool every morning, massaging the buffalo's neck with butter so that a single strike would slice its head off. He was aware that in the past, a buffalo offered by a brahmin family from Maravitha had had to be struck three times. The buffalo had been offered to save the life of the man's son who was suffering from cholera. The boy died.

The sight of Singhadatta sitting on the cane stool, massaging the animal's neck wrenched Bidhibala's heart. She used to wonder if it might be better if she died herself. She had seriously considered placing her own head on the sacrificial altar.

Once again, the words stabbed at Singhadatta's ears, like a dagger. "Drag him out! He knows where the buffalo is."

"I, Singhadatta will bring two buffaloes for the ten-armed goddess instead of one. Leave. All of you, go away!"

Part of the crowd dispersed. But the majority stayed on under the dimaru tree in front of Manomohan's house. They were waiting for more action.

Singhadatta paced the courtyard. He gesticulated wildly, shouting all the while, "Why did we come here? Wasn't there any other head priest in Nilachal?" He grabbed the sacred thread across his chest, shouting, "I had promised to sacrifice a buffalo. Now I vow to offer two buffaloes to the goddess. I will sell my land if I have to. I swear ..."

He started banging his head against the wooden posts. The house shook as though it had been struck by an earthquake. The two midgets had joined the gathering in front of Manomohan Sarma's house. With disproportionately large heads, they appeared somewhat grotesque. They were like Tal-Betal in the mythical court of Vikramaditya.

The midgets had grown up in the temple and had assumed special roles. They carried messages for the head priests, caused rifts between the priests, and also, trapped and sold the doves set free by the devotees. The two little men waddled through the crowd in gamochas and tattered vests, promising, "We'll fix up the buffaloes in a matter of two hours."

A tantrik came forward, stick in hand. A skull was secured to one end of the stick. He wore only a small red loincloth. Though his skin was fair, it was marked, as if he had leucoderma. His hair was a dull red. His eyes were sunk deep in their sockets. He pushed his way through the crowd and tried making his point with gestures. The crowd deduced that he must have committed some cardinal sin, like killing a brahmin or a cow. No one could decipher his stance – whether he was against animal sacrifice or not. The hubbub rose again. This time Singhadatta roared, "I give Ratnadhar three hours to bring back the buffalo. I shall bathe the feet of the ten-armed goddess with the buffalo's blood."

The crowd could almost see the river of blood. The two midgets broke into a gleeful little jig. "Singhadatta, call the buffaloes by the names of your enemies and hack them in two. Make sure that Sikdar does not have to strike twice. Hold the severed head – with a flaming lamp inside – and stand in front of the goddess for one full day and night. Then you will be king."

Singhadatta shouted to his son over the din, "Hoi Rudra, bring me my umbrella and stick. I shall cross the river right now and get the buffaloes." The old house shuddered as he stomped around the veranda. Bishnupriya came out and pleaded tearfully with Singhadatta.

"You cannot leave like this. You haven't eaten a thing."

"You expect me to eat, after all this? I shall offer the sacrifice to the Almighty Mother today."

There was a commotion inside. Bidhibala, who had never dared raise her head in her father's presence, came out. Eyes blazing, she stormed up to him. "You cannot get buffaloes. You will not bring buffaloes. I shall not marry a man already ..." Singhadatta, furious at his daughter's audacity, lost control and threw his khadau, the wooden slipper he was wearing, at her. Bidhibala yelped in pain.

Bishnupriya, with the maid and Rudra, managed to catch her as she fell. Stubbornly she picked herself up. "You will not sacrifice a buffalo. You will not ..."

It was impossible to make Singhadatta see sense. As Singhadatta was leaving, Ratnadhar came out onto the veranda. "If the girl doesn't want to get married, why sacrifice the buffaloes at all? If no one marries Bidhibala, I shall marry her!"

There was a moment of stunned silence. Bishnupriya caught Ratnadhar's hand, pulling him back into the house. She pleaded to the assembly below, "Go and call him! Call Ratnadhar's father. Our guest will pick up the axe ... Call him ..."

Singhadatta roared back, "Ratnadhar! Didn't you go crazy once? Haven't you felt the effect of the goddess' wrath? You have tarnished your religion, living with that white woman. You should be repenting for your sins by performing the Chandaldyanna Bhakshan Prayaschittam. How dare you eye my daughter! You are the one behind the buffalo's disappearance. You will die."

Bishnupriya couldn't take anymore. This was the first time that the people of Bamunpara – the brahmin settlements – heard her speak.

"Singhadatta of Sualkuchi! How dare you insult my son! Look at my hands. I have cooked for the pilgrims all my life. The goddess knows this. How dare you abuse my son! I curse you ..."

Singhadatta's old mother rushed up to Bishnupriya. Taking her hands, she pleaded, "Don't curse him, please. We have already suffered enough. Rudra's brother died. Singhadatta has lost his mind."

Singhadatta went inside and started throwing their belongings together. Rudra followed him, "What are you doing, what are you up to?"

Bidhibala, huddled in a corner began to wail, "I am not going ..."

Singhadatta looked at Bidhibala. Without a word he grabbed her hair and began to kick her viciously. Bishnupriya tried to pull him off. But he was too strong. He flung her aside.

Bidhibala's grandmother was screaming. "You will kill her! She's only a child ... Go my girl, go. Happiness is not written in your destiny. The lord does not will it."

The commotion brought in more people. Dambaru and Rudra grabbed Singhadatta's arms and dragged him off Bidhibala. "Bring her. Rudra called to his grandmother over his shoulder. We shall go to our priest."

"Where are you going? Ratnadhar's father is not back from the temple yet. I beseech you. I apologize!" Bishnupriya pleaded. Nobody was listening.

Rudra signalled the two servants to bring out their belongings. They loaded the luggage on their shoulders and marched down the road. Rudra led, holding his father's hands. Bidhibala followed, still wailing. The crowd, relishing every moment, tagged along, rather like the devotees who followed the deodhas of the goddesses as they raced towards the temple of Mahadev during Deodhwani.

An air of anticipation prevailed.

Dorothy Brown and Chhinnamasta Jatadhari would be arriving in a day or two.

With every passing day, the crowd in front of the Chhinnamasta temple seemed to swell. Different people, different aspirations. In the crowd were three young men from the north bank. They had a friend with them. Dejected, lost, dazed. His thick, dusty hair was parted in the centre. He wore a loose vest and a dhuti. They sat him down on a huge rock in front of the temple. Meanwhile, the Tal-Betal midgets joined them. One stepped forward to take a closer look. But the young man did not look up. His eyes were fixed on the ground. His limbs were stiff.

A devotee asked, "What's wrong with this young man?"

The friends were reluctant. Finally, one blurted out, "We are Safa Khamor, people from the banks of river Manah, a tributary of Brahmaputra. This boy was engaged to a girl from Burhi Khamar. but now she doesn't want to marry him. The boy has stopped eating. Maybe the jatadhari can do something. He once revived a dying marriage."

A disciple cut in, "He will have to meditate on the Chamunda shloka one hundred and eight times. I could teach you."

Two men who were sitting a little further off, joined the circle around him saying, "We are from Hudukhuta Fatemabad in Barpeta district. We have come to the Almighty Mother to free ourselves of fear and grief."

"Fear and grief?"

"We have won the civil case for our land. Now we have been getting death threats from the other party. We are forever in fear of being attacked."

Another devotee asked, "So you have come here to win over your enemies!"

"Yes, yes."

The devotee was rubbing his hands and feet as he recited shlokas of subjugation. Everyone turned to him. Listen, afflict your enemy with disease. That way, neither will the snake sting, nor the stick break. There are still men like Kumaril Bhatt who can inflict disease with the Bhagandar shloka. Why shouldn't there be! An ascetic came up from the Ashwaklanta embankment. When he asked for a coin with the queen's stamp on it, I gave him one. In front of my eyes, he took some ash from his waistband and set fire to it. The copper coin turned gold. The man disappeared in the morning. Here, look, I still have the gold coin."

The devotee's face was covered by a heavy shawl. He made no effort to lift it even as he spoke. Meanwhile, a few more people gathered around him. He regaled them with his anecdotes. "Take some dove-droppings, oil extracted from seeds of the bitter gourd, a donkey's bones and the root of the mayur creeper. Grind them to a smooth paste. Apply it on your enemy's forehead. Wait and see – your enemy's face will shine like the ten heads of Ravana."

The audience burst into laughter.

"If you want to turn your enemy into a cat, put some seeds of the era plant in a black cat's mouth and plant those seeds in black soil. Once it grows, pick the seeds and grind them to a paste. Apply it on your enemy's face, and it will change into a cat's face."

Once again, everyone tittered. One of the disciples shouted, "Sir, you seem to be a top ranking officer. You should think of turning professional."

"Well, I learnt almost all the Kamratna Tantra shlokas from the hermit from Torsa. But the man suddenly disappeared."

"He disappeared after the assault on the white woman. He used to extract the juice from pomegranate seeds on the evening of the Ashlesha Nakshatra, one of the twenty seven signs of the vedic lunar zodiac. On the eighth day after the full moon, he would collect lotus roots and grind them up. Then he would add the juice of the pomegranate seeds to the paste, and apply it to his eyes. He is supposed to have seen visions."

"What did he see?" asked the crowd enthralled.

"The cave of carnal desire inside a ring of smoke. The size of this cave is twenty one fingers. It is red, shaped like a stone womb. In this womb, he said he saw the glorious elemental form of the great goddess Kamakhya."

"Glory be to the Universal Mother, glory be to the Bhashmashailanugamini, glory be to the ten-armed goddess," chanted the devotees.

"This mysterious cave of carnal desire was not the only vision he had. He saw the other sacred sites of the goddesses as well.

His eyes were dazzled. The footprints of the ten-armed goddess marked everything.

"Her hair was black as a moonless Amabasya night. She was soaked in blood. She commanded the hermit, Bring buffaloes for sacrifice. Deliver human blood to the crematorium where I live. Wash my feet with the blood of a sinner. He will be absolved of his sins and so will you. Casting aside his human form, the sinner will ascend to a higher level and become lord of the gods. Human blood will keep me satisfied for eight months. Bring me blood. The ascetic heard the clanging of chains around the ankles of the men brought for sacrifice. They hissed like vicious, poisonous snakes."

Tal-Betal, the two temple midgets, set up a wild dance. They chorused sardonically, "Drag the hermit back. If he advocates sacrifice, let him offer blood!"

An elderly devotee got unsteadily to his feet. His dhuti, hitched up to his knees, he said, "We are not here to listen to tales about the hermit from Torsa. We are waiting for the jatadhari. He wants to wipe away the bloodstains from this abode of the Mother. Hundreds, young and old have gathered today. We want to see him!"

"The hermit from Torsa talks about the thousand year old tradition of offering blood. Let him offer his own blood like the scriptures say. Our king's mount is still proof that in this holy abode of Mother Kamakhya, King Narasingha cut off his own head and offered it to the goddess."

The crowd joined in, "Yes, the king cut off his own head with the sacrificial blade and offered it to the Mother on this very pilgrimage."

A student of the tol who had come to collect signatures said,

"King Surath repeatedly marked offerings to the Mother with his own blood." He raised his voice, so everyone could hear. "The hermit from Torsa claims that if sacrifices are stopped, the Mother Goddess will destroy the earth. What about human sacrifice then? Has the world ended with its prohibition?"

A devotee who had come here to meet the jatadhari said, "This holiest of the Mother's holy abodes has survived the fury of the Brahmaputra only because human sacrifice has ended. This land is still green and bountiful. The Mother's blessings have prevailed!"

Tal-Betal shouted over the loud applause, "Go, bring a man for the sacrifice and show us." And they romped cheerfully about. Another devotee posed a question, "But humans shouldn't be replaced by animals. They drag helpless animals to the sacrifice. The Mother has never said that she would reduce the earth's abundance to ashes if she were not offered blood. According to the holy books, flowers are equally acceptable to the Mother. The writings say that anyone making an offering of a thousand karabi flowers and a thousand kunda flowers, will have all his desires fulfilled. Also, he earns the religious merit of living in the abode of the goddess."

Everyone joined in, "A house of flowers. The finest offering!"

The speaker carried away by his own erudition continued, "A devotee who offers prayers with a thousand purple lotuses, earns himself the distinction of being the goddess' companion for a million centuries and lives in the Rudraloka, the kingdom of Lord Shiva.

The sixteenth century tantrik text, the *Yogini Tantra* describes the rituals for Shakti worship in Kamakhya and the other sacred places of Kamarup. It recommends flowers. The status of flowers is higher than blood. The sacred texts state that the goddess is satiated for a hundred years with the blood of a single buffalo. The same writings also claim that an offering of one karabi flower can earn the devotee the virtues of the most arduous yagna, the Ashwamedha or horse sacrifice. Offerings of flowers can earn us the virtues of the Agnishtom sacrifice and secure a place in the land of the sun."

The devotees chorused, "Throw out the blood. Worship the goddess with flowers. Ma ... Ma ... Ma! Human souls are hidden behind a wall of petals. The invisible soul is made fragrant with flowers. The soul, scented with flowers, can pull a victim from the jaws of death."

Inspired, the devotees intoned, "Ma ... Ma!"

Five or six women ran gaily towards the Koutilinga temple. Four well-built men followed, beating their drums. They wore clean dhutis with sandalwood tilaks on their foreheads. Around their necks were garlands that they had received after paying obeisance to the goddess. The devotees waiting for the jatadhari looked up. The women had dusky complexions. Red karabi flowers spilled their fragrance into the air. It was evident that they were prostitutes from Gaur or North Shekhadari. One of them was picking up the empty cartridge shells left behind by the British officers.

"These girls must be from the Kanchi Kumari clan!" Someone said.

Everyone agreed.

Another devotee said, "King Vishambar of the Chaitra dynasty attained salvation by worshipping the dark daughter of a prostitute." A murmur rose among the disciples. Some craned their necks to catch a glimpse of the women. No one could really say where they had come from.

The disciple continued, "True that the prostitute's daughter was dark as the black night, but the king attained salvation by bathing in the mystic light radiating from the virgin's dusky body. Hence the texts state that virgins worshipped in India are imbued with a celestial light. This is what the *Yogini Tantra* says."

Laughter rippled through the crowd. Just then, Singhadatta appeared, walking down towards the embankment, stick in hand, a turban on his head. Behind him was his son, Rudra, marching down carrying a metal trunk. They did not speak.

Tal-Betal piped up, "Singhadatta will buy the buffaloes even if he has to sell his land. The sacrificial altar will be swamped in blood!"

The devotees waiting for the jatadhari lamented, "Oh no! The jatadhari will be here before that and offer a house of flowers to the Mother."

Another disciple joined them. "You can earn greater blessings by offering flowers than by offering blood."

As they spoke, a buffalo being dragged off to the sacrifice altar by some devotee broke loose and ran into the crowd. Scattering clothes and utensils, the buffalo charged down into the valley.

The devotees ran helter-skelter.

The full moon rippled on the Brahmaputra, its silvery image like a fair woman trapped naked underwater.

The women from North Shekhadari, who were living in the Kamakhya caves, came out to watch. Two virgins, here for the Kumari Puja, burst into a spontaneous song.

Oh Mother, a thousand salutations to you,
your river and your moon.
Oh Mother, your river and your moon. "

The women with the virgins took up the refrain,

Oh Mother, your river, your moon.

The drummers pounded their drums. The cymbal players clashed their cymbals. After about an hour of singing, they all went back to their caves. A few boats came to the bank, oars splashing.

The light grew brighter as did the moon's splendour. It was as if the moon had stolen the milky glow of the brahmin-daughters of Kamakhya, and bathed in it before it shimmered in the sky.

Every sixteen year old girl in the holy abode wanted to steal back the moon-skin. Of course they did. Who would want to wear a skin that blemished and ruptured and bled from a hundred places?

As the night grew longer, the hubbub dimmed and so did the rehearsals. The fierce shouts of the devotees were heard, trying to play deodhas of the goddess. The mystery of the night intensified with the deodhas' cries, "Oh! Oh Ma! Oh! Oh Ma Chamunda, Ma Bhairavi!"

The elderly devotees from North Shekhadari were just putting their drums, metal trunks, clothes and other belongings aside to sort out their sleeping mats and bedspreads for the night. A drummer saw the shadow fall across the house nearest the cave. "Who's there? The girls screamed."

Some stranger, radiant as light! The moonlight, like a silver veil, cascaded down her hair.

An elderly woman hobbled out with an earthen lamp. She saw someone standing there.

The other girls warned, "Don't go any further bai."

"Who's that?" asked the old woman.

The girl's complexion seemed to radiate light. She did not flinch. The elderly woman raised the lamp. She was startled. She had never seen a face so beautiful.

"Oh! Why should you be standing outside? Come in, come in."

She grabbed the girl's arms and almost dragged her to the house in front of the cave. Shooing away the curious girls she pulled the stranger to a corner, asked, "Where are you from? The north bank, or Upper Assam?"

The girl stared at her vacantly.

"Fine. What is your name?"

Silence.

"Are you a brahmin?"

She nodded.

"So?"

The young girl was still staring at the old woman's face. This time the woman raised her voice, "Why are you here then?"

She took the girl's hand. Slowly, step by step, they entered the house in front of the cave. Inside, between the drummers and the girls there was utter confusion. The elderly woman had accommodated the two virgins brought for Kumari Puja in this room. Garlands of karabi and marigolds lay scattered all over the floor.

She shouted, "Clean up! Clean up the room. All these garlands of marigold and wood apple leaves are the goddess' blessings, touch them to your head. And look at these girls. They've been brought for the Kumari Puja, but they wouldn't budge from the theatre." Then, she addressed the new woman, "Sit down dear! Sit down."

Once again, the woman looked inquisitively at the girl's face. It wasn't that such things had not happened before. Not so long ago a brahmin widow had come to their house in Shekhadari. She was from the Boko side. She had been raped and was carrying her attacker's child. The poor woman had appointed a lawyer in Gauhati to fight a case over her land. He took advantage of her. Before that, there had been the incident of a pregnant brahmin widow from Dakhla, seeking shelter in the Macchkhova Muslim settlement. Everybody heard about it.

Meanwhile, a crowd had formed at her doorstep. The elderly woman clapped her hands to shoo the girls away. Then she suddenly ripped the chadar from the girl's breast. She wore nothing under her blouse. Before the girl realized what was happening, the woman with the speed of lightning, tore off her blouse. Her eyes fell on two soft mounds.

Two mounds of turbulence that could sink a loaded boat in the Brahmaputra. Two mounds of flesh that could shake the foundations of empire!

She called to the girls, "Come! Come and behold the beauty of breasts, yet untouched by man!"

By now, dawn was breaking. Clumps of cloud, painted in shades of black and red, had gathered over Bhasmachal. They looked like parts of Sati's body, lying across Shiva's shoulders. Parts, sliced off by Brahma, Vishnu and Shani. Yes, the gods had blown away the rest of the body after the feet, thighs, womb, navel, breasts, shoulders and neck had fallen on different parts of the country. Those red clouds, blowing away, looked like the other parts of Sati's body, which had flown away to be immersed in the celestial Ganga.

Crowds were gathering in front of the cave. The drummers, the harmonium and tabla players had by now squeezed through the door. A group of devotees waiting for the jatadhari also tried to take a peek, but the woman standing guard cried out, "There is nobody here. Get away! Get lost you rascals!"

The head woman went out to spit out her chewed betel nut. When she came back, she wagged a finger and enunciated carefully, "Not a soul must hear of this. Do you understand?"

Everybody chorused, "Yes, we understand."

Like every other day, the white men had gathered for shooting practice in the forest at sunrise.

With the onset of monsoons, the trees had closed in. The sculpted crowns of the bheleu trees were heavy with green blossoms. Gulmohar and moroi were in full bloom. The stalks of the bhatghila, were pregnant with seed – like eggs in a lizard's belly shown up by the sun. The round gandhasoroi leaves shone like coins stamped with the queen's seal. Sam and jackfruit leaves swayed towards each other in play. The forest was filled with squirrel-tailed zari leaves. And in the branches, chattering monkeys brightened up the damp green of the forest.

Like on every other day, the white men roamed the forest. They saw some boats in the distance. One approached from the opposite direction. As the boat anchored, two buffaloes were offloaded amidst confusion. The white men watched them force the reluctant buffaloes up the slope. They heard the loud shouts from the goddess' holy abode. A group of priests, the local troubleshooters, rushed down the path below Bhuvaneshwari, towards the white men. Clad in red dhutis, their shirt pockets bulged with the papers of their pilgrim devotees. Panting hard they asked, "Sir! You come here before dawn. A girl is missing. Have you seen a brahmin girl from a good family!"

"Girl ... a young girl?" The tall strapping white man had a gun in his hand.

"Yes. A young girl from Sualkuchi," chorused the two priests.

A small white man rushed out from behind the trees. "I came here with the munshi last night. One of my revolvers was missing. Something strange was going on."

"What?"

"I heard the splashing of oars, so I looked towards the river. A boat had come in. It was full moon and the whole area was bright as day. A group of people tumbled down the slope. A piece of the hill had slid down. They were in a hurry to board the boat. Within minutes it splashed away into the fog."

"It must have been them!"

The priests scrambled up as if they had found a major clue. The month of Shravana was coming to a close. From the first day of this month, the deodha installed the deity outside his house and offered prayers to it every day. During the whole month, the deodhas stayed away from their daily routine. They left the house every evening. At their deity's bidding they wandered around the temple complex through the night.

The darkness grew sinister with the cries of men possessed by the goddess as her deodha. "Oh! Oh! Mai! Mai! Mai! Mai! Oh Mai Chamunda! Oh Mai Tara!"

Children woke in terror. So many deodhas of the gods and

goddesses: Kamakhya, Mahadev, Chhinnamasta, Samshan Kali, Manasa, Chalanta, Bhuvaneshwari, Bagala, Ganesh, Narayan, the deodha of Maharaj. Sometimes the men who came to play the deodhas wove through the crowd and suddenly prostrated themselves on the ground. Clad in the bare minimum, their bodies were sprinkled with red sendur.

As the priests scaled the slope, a deodha from Gaur brushed past them. "This deodha is a Muslim from Gaur," said the priest in front. "But, I'm certain he won't be able to take the grilling."

"There was a Muslim devotee last year as well. He claimed to be Kali's deodha. Don't you remember! But he couldn't go on," said the other priest. "Apparently, when a group of deodhas interviewed him by the side of the Soubhagya Kunda, the goddess left him."

The priests saw a large crowd gathering down below at the river embankment. There was a major rush. Shoving the priests aside, some devotees ran down the slope. In the confusion, notes and papers fell out of the priests' bulging pockets. As they hurriedly gathered up their papers, they heard a commotion. The words reverberated on the hillsides:

Chhinnamasta Jatadhari has returned ...

Chhinnamasta Jatadhari has returned ...

The priests muttered to each other, "A serious matter. The sons of the purohits, the head priests and the acolytes have joined hands. The wretched man is trying to bring to an end a system that has endured for a thousand years! His disciples even dare to ask how human sacrifice came to an end!"

"Doesn't that wretched man know that blood after all, is blood, be it human or goat! Anyway, Singhadatta is back, with the buffaloes! But where is the girl?"

There was an uproar near the Soubhagya Kunda. Singhadatta Sarma was shouting at the top of his voice, "Where's the girl? How can she just disappear? Where is my daughter?"

The steps around the Soubagya Kunda were packed with people. Former deodhas were cross-examining a boy from the Hajo area who claimed he was possessed by the Goddess Bagala.

Two fathers of schoolboys from Dakhala and Urput claiming to have been possessed like deodhas, had spent the whole night sitting on the Soubhagya Kunda steps. Oddly enough, both boys displayed identical behaviour. They had stopped eating for quite some time. The boy from Urput who never touched meat, suddenly caught grabbed a pair of pet doves, broke their necks and drank their blood. He spent all his time shouting, "Oh Ma! Oh Ma!" around the Bhairavi temple. The women of the house sat in their courtyards and sang hymns to Shiva:

Look, open your eyes and look ye lord of the crematorium.

But to no avail. In order to calm their rising passion, both fathers had even sought out an old deodha and had acquired talismans for their sons, so the boys could go back to their schools. Nothing worked.

The rush of devotees increased. Today, countless goats had been brought for sacrifice. The goats were tied up on the veranda of the house in front of the sacrificial altar. The blood from the goats that were sacrificed, spattered all over the living goats as well.

Everyone looked up when they heard Singhadatta. Breaking through the crowd and stepping over the aspiring deodhas, Singhadatta rushed down.

A new man from Hajo who had come to be the deodha of Ma Kali was causing a huge furore in front of the Kali temple. His eyes were bloodshot. His long hair was plastered with sweat. His body was covered in dust and he was drooling. He was bewildered by the grilling he was getting at the hands of the former deodhas.

"Where is the abode of the Goddess Kali?"

Ma Kali's favourite haunt is the crematorium!" His reply was instant.

"Describe the goddess."

"Dark, with a garland of skulls, open tresses, and blood red tongue. Three bloodshot eyes. The scriptures have stated that the war-loving yoginis sprang from her brilliant aura. At the origin of time, there arose one million universes from the root of every hair in her body. The Universal Mother sucked in the vicious monsters with her long tongue and devoured them, along with the entire universe!"

"Devoured them?"

"Yes, chewed them up."

The boy from Hajo now rolled on the ground with flailing hands and feet. As he thrashed about, he called out, "Ma ... Ma ... Raise a red flag to the Mother. Bring a black goat for the Mother. I shall slit it with my teeth. Beat the drum for the Mother." He got up suddenly and threaded his way through the crowd. Pushing aside Singhadatta, who had come in search of Bidhibala, he ran up the steps.

Meanwhile, news of Bidhibala's disappearance had reached the head priest. He wasted no time sending men to the valley and to the other embankments – Kameshwar, Siddheswari, Amratakeshwar.

The boat carrying the jatadhari moved slowly ahead. It had a saffron flag on its mast and the earthen pot trimmed with wood apple leaves was prominent at the bow. His devotees were singing hymns to the accompaniment of drums and cymbals. A throng of students were waiting, with lotus garlands and karabi flowers. A student from the tol shouted, "If we are welcoming the jatadhari straight from the river, we must offer him a seat made of stone, kusha grass or wood. The scriptures state that in order to worship Durga, a seat of stone, bones or wood is appropriate. Listen, not any other bones but an elephant's. Seats of iron, bronze and lead are also not appropriate.

"Ratnadhar, you must have read the shloka that says, seats made of gold embedded with pearls are useless to an ascetic. Wood, bones, cloth and cotton are more than adequate for a hermit." And he started reciting the shloka,

Na yathshasana bhuyat
Pujakarmani sadhakah
Kasthadikasanani bhuyat
Sitameva sada budhah.

Ratnadhar was very excited. He couldn't wait to fall at the feet of the jatadhari. The very thought left him in a state of reverent stupor. He remembered the need for a seat just as the red and saffron flags on the mast of the boat came into his line of vision. He will have to listen to his disciples sitting on the bank. He will go up by this Swargadwar. This is the north gate, the gate of liberation. The jatadhari would recite the ascension mantra from this very point.

Gradually, the crowd grew in strength. There was bedlam amongst the ranks of disciples. A couple of drummers who had come early to Kamakhya for the Deodhwani, began beating their drums. The groups of women Namatis from Mirza and Palasbari began to wail.

Ratnadhar ran up to fetch a seat for the jatadhari. By then, the news of Bidhibala's disappearance had spread like wildfire. Singhadatta, with Dambaru and Rudra, searched frantically all over for her. They looked in Natpara, Hemtola, Bamunpara, Bezpara, Napitpara. Then he came down to the bank, followed by Rudra, Dambaru and others.

Hands and feet flapping in rage, he roared at the crowd, "Where is Ratnadhar?"

"*He* is behind Bidhibala's disappearance! Ratnadhar! Where are you, you swine!"

The students from the tol were terror struck. He couldn't find Ratnadhar in the crowd. So Singhadatta raced up to a dilapidated temple and barged into rehearsal. A burly man, playing Kalapahar, was repeating his lines, "I have used Shree Ramchandra's khadau to pluck wood apples from the trees. I have used broken pieces of temple idols to weigh meat. I have performed wood consecration on the Murshidabad streets, lighting the fire with the wooden idols of Jagannath from the Puri temple. I! I ..."

The actor held an aggressive pose, waving a prop machete similar to the ones used for human sacrifice. It was just then that Singhadatta Sarma made a dramatic entry. Without bothering to excuse himself, he searched every corner, to check if Ratnadhar was hiding anywhere. The actor shouted back at him, "What are you doing? We are a performing troupe from Srirampur. We are not in the habit of hiding fugitives."

He went over to the two youngsters rehearsing with Shahbanu Begum and the others, and lifted up their chunnis with the tip of his foil covered wooden sabre for Singhadatta to see.

Singhadatta pushed through the crowd and left, Rudra and Dambaru scurrying after him. They were agitated. Who knows

... who can say ... Singhadatta would surely kill someone today! No one could stop him.

Stomping through the crowd of devotees that had assembled for the Deodhwani, at intervals Singhadatta thundered, "Where is Bidhibala?"

As luck would have it, Ratnadhar was totally unaware of any danger. Accompanied by a few students of the tol, he was walking down the slope, carrying a brightly painted wooden seat for the jatadhari on his head. Ratandhar had no idea that Bidhibala was missing.

A loud commotion broke out on the Mekhela-Ujuwa path. Singhadatta pounced on Ratnadhar, sending the wooden seat flying. As Rudra tried desperately to pull him off, Singhadatta began to kick and punch him. The devotees were in an uproar. Singhadatta and his quarry looked like they were about to roll down the hill in spite of all efforts to separate them. Singhadatta seemed to have acquired superhuman strength. He had assumed the form of a predator out for the kill. He was convinced that it was this boy and no other, who could be responsible for Bidhibala's disappearance. Ratnadhar was covered in blood. He dragged him to the centre of the devotees waiting for the jatadhari. The students from the tol tried their best to get their friend away from Singhadatta's vice grip. "What has he done? You will kill him." They shouted desperately trying to drive some sense into the crazed Singhadatta.

Just then, the jatadhari's boat reached the bank. An agonized cry ripped through the chaos. It seemed to split the sky. For a moment, everything seemed to stand still.

The jatadhari set foot on the bank. The women devotees broke into a loud wail. The sound of blowing conches merged with clashing cymbals. The jatadhari stood on the riverbank. The fearsome dreadlocks on his head – the colour of soil from the holy abode streaked with dry sacrificial blood – as if braided with deadly serpents. He appeared to have put on weight. His eyes flashed with some sort of divine light. Behind this veil of light there was quiet displeasure mixed with coldness and reproach.

Breaking the wall of devotees, the jatadhari pulled Ratnadhar from the deadly grip, flinging Singhadatta aside. "Ratnadhar is my disciple," he roared. "He cannot do such a thing." Our boat crossed your daughter's boat about twenty five thousand cubits from here. A disciple of mine from Sualkuchi who was with me was astonished to see your daughter Bidhibala, in the company of prostitutes from North Shekhadari!"

The disciple from Sualkuchi came forward to substantiate the statement, "I saw Bidhibala. She was standing with the girls at the helm of the boat with her hair open!"

The jatadhari lifted Ratnadhar's limp, unconscious body, and marched off. His disciples followed suit. Singhadatta Sarma fell down on the ground in a dead faint.

D rummers from Kaihati, Palashbari, Datkuchi, Borkheti – even from as far off as Darrang's Satgharia Bordoulguri and Matia of Goalpara – rushed into the temporary camps at the Kamakhya peeth. The privileged ones, who were legal occupants at Kamakhya, took their positions. Most wore black. Some wore long sleeved shirts. A couple were wearing faded coats. A handful flaunted Gandhi caps. The Gandhi topi was becoming popular around that time.

Two Karka drummers, wearing cat and fox masks were performing acrobatics in the forecourt below. Tal-Betal followed them like shadows. Nobody could turn somersaults better than the drummers. Devotees arriving for the Deodhwani rushed in to watch them. With every spin, the crowd cheered. The temple complex resounded to the sound of drumbeats and clashing cymbals.

Since the drummers' travel expenses were borne by the temple committee, they were happy to come. They walked half the distance and travelled the rest by bullock cart. During their stay they would partake of the temple food-offerings. They received two dhutis from the priest and one from the treasurer. A set of clothes would also come from the goddess' peeth. They would also be flooded with coins.

An old deodha from North Shekhadari sat on the steps of the Chhinnamasta temple. Last year, he had been barred from the dance. He had dragged the girl who washed the sacrificial altar to a Bhatghila tree and assaulted her. There had been a great uproar the next morning. A tumour was now growing in his stomach. He used to work as a blacksmith but now he begged for alms. Though he covered himself from head to foot, people still recognized him, for his head was abnormally large. His hair stood on end, stiff as a sprouting plant. His bare feet were so rough that they no longer looked like human feet.

Meanwhile, the pitcher dedicated to the Goddess Manasa was placed on an eight-petalled lotus in the amphitheatre. The task of daubing the pitcher with sendur, turmeric and panchapallav leaves – peepal, bakul, bamboo and others, was already on. People waited in the forecourt of the amphitheatre, to make offerings to the eight serpents. Grapefruit, coconuts, and marigolds flooded the arena where the Goddess Manasa, adorned with white flowers, was installed. In the centre, the deadly golden cobra, raised its hood. Flanking her were two silver snakes, upright, hoods flared, as if dancing. Two other serpents towered over the goddess, their hoods forming her crown.

One story went that during the Burmese invasion, a goldsmith from Loharghat had buried a pot full of gold in his backyard. A member of the Bharali family had stumbled on the pot and had used the gold to make the cobra for the goddess. Another version was that someone from the Bharali family had killed the snake that guarded the pot. When serpents began to invade the dreams of some members of the family, they had commissioned the golden serpent and offered it to the Goddess Manasa.

And those stones in the goddess' eyes. How they glittered! A canopy of flowers shaded her. The deodhas sat near the sacrificial altar. The devotees were falling over each other to lie at their feet, to get a glimpse of the future.

Meanwhile, the jatadhari took leave of his followers and prepared to go to Manomohan's house. The devotees had stayed with him until the wee hours of the morning. As soon as they left, he went down to the Brahmaputra. As usual, no one could say which part of the river he would disappear into. It was rumoured that he swam all the way to Umananda, in the centre of the Brahmaputra.

The path was littered with empty cartridges. They were clear indication that more and more white men were coming here for rifle practice. The independence movement was fast gaining ground. The white men were growing cautious. Volunteers were prepared to lay down their lives for the motherland. Mahatma Gandhi had launched a war of emotions where moral issues took the place of bullets.

The movement for independence gathered momentum when the Mahatma visited Gauhati to raise funds in August 1921. It is said that the great scholar Hem Chandra Goswami had quizzed the Mahatma on the immortal books, Hastirvidyarnaba and Katha

Geeta. He had said, "You once wrote that the Assamese are stupid, ignorant and uncouth people."

Mahatma Gandhi was taken aback. It was true that he had written this. But now he was amazed at the scholarship and dedication within the community. Even nursing mothers removed jewellery from their hands and ears and donated it to the cause of swaraj. Gandhi was profuse in his apologies.

The jatadhari splashed out of the water.

As he ascended the slope, every now and again a cry tore from the depths of his heart, "Ma! Ma! Glory be to you Ma! Glory be to you! Ma Rudreshwari! Ma Mahakali Kamakhya! Ma Chhinnamasta! Ma! Ma!"

The jatadhari wrapped himself in the pat silk chadar presented by his disciples and left for Manomohan's house. No one had ever known the jatadhari to visit a priest's house before. Whole families trooped out onto their verandas to gape. A stream of devotees followed him. Most of them were from the tol.

The ascetic had ministered to Ratnadhar with shlokas and medicine before lifting him on his shoulders to carry him home. Murmuring an inaudible mantra, he stopped short at the door. An old woman from Malipara sat at Ratnadhar's head, singing a shloka to relieve the pain.

One by one, members of Manomohan's family filed out. Ratnadhar had been sent to Gauhati in a temple palanquin for treatment. Fortunately, though his head was still bandaged, there were no broken ribs. He tried to sit up when he was told that the jatadhari had come. Manomohan greeted the jatadhari. A large wooden pira was placed by the bed. Devotees and students waited outside.

The Soubhagya Kunda was clearly visible from the house. The deodhas sat in a row on the side of the tank, waiting for the ritual purification to begin. The cloths round their waists looked like the pelts of sacrificed animals. Some had hair growing down to their shoulders. Others had tonsured heads. While still others wore spiky cropped hair, the colour of earth mixed with dried blood. Some had gamochas over their shoulders, others had left their chests bare. The head priest was there as well. A devotee pointed to the tallest deodha. He was from Hudu Khata near Fatemabad. An old deodha. He had once nearly died of cholera. It was rumoured that in the throes of the disease, he had acquired divine strength and begun to dance. The goddess had blessed him with a new lease of life. He was easily recognizable from the red hibiscus flower tied to the end of his long hair.

Ratnadhar leaned forward to clasp the jatadhari's knees. His mother stood by the ascetic's side, sobbing. "He was getting better, but lately he has been muttering in his sleep. Where is Bidhibala? Where is Bidhibala? Who put this curse on me?"

Bishnupriya broke down.

With his arm around Ratnadhar, the jatadhari reassured Bishnupriya, "Nothing will happen. If it had been serious, they would not have discharged him from the hospital. They've sent him home, haven't they? There is no reason to worry."

Bishnupriya pursed her lips. "If anything happens to my son," she said slowly, "I shall curse ... Ma Chhinnamasta knows the state of my hands. I shall put a curse on Singhadatta."

The jatadhari said soothingly, "Today, Ratnadhar will try to walk."

Manomohan Sarma took the jatadhari aside. "Be careful," he whispered. "I overheard them talking near the amphitheatre. They are planning to drag all those who oppose animal sacrifice to the altar and offer them to the goddess. They were instructing Goddess Bogola's deodha. The deodhas are roaming around making a big commotion. Have you heard them calling to the Mother in the temple forecourt? Their heads are covered with coloured powder and sendur."

The jatadhari raised his eyes and looked squarely at Ratnadhar's father, "What are you trying to tell me?"

"People are in awe of the deodhas. They believe that causing them any sort of stress will invite the goddess' wrath."

"Yes, I am aware of that. But ...?"

"I have also been told that some devotee has stuck a dagger in the waistband of Shamshan Kali's deodha. As you know, deodhas of the goddesses do not abide by any rules or laws. So much so that they don't deem it necessary to observe even the basic rituals associated with birth and death."

He continued. "Do you remember the deodha of Chhinnamasta from Shekhadari three years ago? He cremated his mother, then came straight to the sacrificial altar, drank the blood of a black goat that had just been sacrificed and began to dance. No one dared to protest."

The jatadhari got up to leave. "I still don't understand. What are you trying to tell me Manomohan."

"The dagger could find its way to your heart ..."

The jatadhari hurried off. A parrot, the colour of the plantain leaf, flew down to perch on his shoulder. The waiting students and devotees followed behind him.

Word was about that a powerful lobby was planning an attack on members of the anti-animal sacrifice movement. The temple priests and clerks, men both young and old were gathering at the Bhairavi and Bhubaneshwari temples for a secret conclave. Even their children had joined the congregation. Those who secretly admired the jatadhari were concerned that he had returned. Shambhu, the machete-man, was probably the first person to move the courts regarding the mismanagement of temple funds by the priests. Now he had also joined this secret conclave.

The pro-sacrifice lobby conspired while cutting the plantain leaves on which the deodhas would be seated for their ceremonial investiture. The deodhas were dressed in new robes and adorned with sendur, sacrificial blood, and a headdress made of wood apple leaves. They carried sendur smeared wooden swords in their hands. Would the swords they carried this year be fake? Or real? If a possessed deodha sliced someone to ribbons in a violent frenzy – would anyone protest?

The jatadhari emerged from a secret chamber in the temple. The students formed a protective ring around him. A herd of male goats with sendur marks on their foreheads were grazing by the path leading to the Goddess Manasa at the amphitheatre. "These goats have been dedicated by Muslim devotees from Shekhadari and Bankura," said a young man. "Animal offerings made by Muslim devotees are not beheaded."

They watched the jatadhari gently stroking a goat. "See how happily they play," he said. "How they come to us when we call. They are intelligent beings."

Turning to face the golden dome of the temple, he raised his arms. "Ma ... Ma ... Ma ..."

Very softly he said to the devotees, "These are pure, beautiful, innocent lives. Put your ear to their breast and you will hear the footsteps of Ma Kamakhya. Listen for yourselves. Listen to the Mother's footsteps. The same rhythm that beats in your own breast!"

He walked up to a goat and put an ear to its flank. Goat bells clanged. The jatadhari continued, "Listen. O faithful, just as our mothers want us to live and be happy – so does the Goddess Kamakhya want her children to live and be happy. Gather round, O Hindu and Muslim devotees, wash the bloodstains from this beautiful earth. Hail to you."

Meanwhile, the crowd grew around the jatadhari. Doves fluttered up to him to settle on his dreadlocks. A man with a headdress of wood apple leaves, sendur all over his body, appeared out of nowhere. He broke through the throng of devotees surrounding the jatadhari. A fracas broke out. He shot off like a bullet towards the Soubhagya Kunda. The doves rose from the jatadhari's shoulders in a flurry of flapping wings. The devotees clung to the jatadhari, like the doves to the temple.

A young man with note pads full of signatures said, "That was Kali's deodha. He drank blood and smeared his body with it. He had a dagger under his gamocha."

"A dagger ...?"

The jatadhari walked on with his disciples. They saw four deodhas smoking ganja near the sacrificial altar. Where had they come from – North Shekhadari, Loharghat, or Barihat? They were sweating profusely. From time to time devotees fell at their feet. The deodhas would bless them with perspiration soaked wood apple leaves, exclaiming, "Hai Mai! Hai Mai!"

The hills reverberated with salutations to the Goddess Manasa.

"Oh Ma Manasa. Oh Ma bedecked with serpents."

The jatadhari stopped by the amphitheatre. The students made sure he was surrounded. In the eerie light of the earthen lamps the idol of the Goddess Manasa looked fearsome. It was shrouded by hundreds of doves smeared with turmeric and sendur. A pile of lifeless goat heads lay at the goddess' feet. Deodhas, exhausted by the constant dancing, would occasionally dart off to the sacrificial altar for a few puffs of ganja. Then they would prostrate themselves before the goddess. Before rising, they would stretch their arms and poke around in the mound of flowers, the goat heads and the roosting doves. An inebriated devotee fell flat on his face. Someone tried to help him up and carry him outside.

The drums grew louder. Hymns in praise of Manasa sounded over the cacophony. The mound of goat heads grew higher. A tantrik in red pushed through the crowd. A trickle of sweat ran down his back. His eyes spewed fire. Pointing melodramatically at the jatadhari, he croaked, "Sinner! He tries to choke the goddess' thirst for blood ... A great sinner!"

The jatadhari was unfazed. The circle of students tightened around him.

There was a bloodcurdling scream from the direction of the altar: "Drag him by the dreadlocks!"

The dancing deodhas broke their rhythm for a quick puff of ganja at the sacrificial altar. This was the moment when devotees would fall at their feet to seek solutions to their problems or cures for incurable diseases. A scuffle broke out. Each wanted to be the first one to grasp the deodhas' feet.

Pushing their way through the throng, the jatadhari and the students left. It was time for him to go down to the riverbank. Dorothy Brown was to arrive today. A knot of priests and tantriks near the sacrificial altar were watching them intently. Their glares were sharp as daggers. The stench of blood was overpowering.

The deodha of Shamshan Kali leaned against the sacrificial

altar, taking deep pulls at a chillum. The sacrificial blood, sendur and sweat all merged in a sticky rivulet down his back. A devotee dragged a black goat up to the altar. Face down before the deodha, he dedicated the goat, pleading for release from some terminal disease. The deodha handed his chillum of ganja to a bystander, took off his garland, and wiping down the sweat, sendur and bloodstains with it, gave it to the devotee. "Worship this garland and you will be cured ..."

Then, without warning, the deodha sank his teeth into the goat's neck. As the goat bleated, struggling to free itself, drops of blood fell on the ground. No one there had ever seen anything like this before.

They heard shouting from the students encircling the jatadhari. A blade flashed, a knife lodged itself in the jatadhari's dreadlocks. In the ensuing bedlam, the students swiftly led the jatadhari through the Hanumandwar.

The students were agitated. "It was a plot hatched by the pro-sacrifice group. A conspiracy! They're out to kill the jatadhari!"

Hail Ma Shamshan Kali. The jatadhari raised his hands skywards, reassuring them. "Do not panic. Taking life is not easy. Those trying to wipe out this bloody ritual must be prepared to sacrifice their own blood."

Inspired, the students chorused, "Yes. Those trying to stop blood being spilled must not be afraid to sacrifice their own blood."

The setting sun glinted off the river – as if some mystery woman had just dipped her golden tresses into the water. A canopied boat snaked its way towards the embankment.

News of Dorothy Brown's return had spread. A crowd had already gathered near the embankment. The jatadhari extracted the knife from his dreadlocks and flung it into the profound depths of the Brahmaputra. Then he washed his hands in the river. The students closed in around him.

There were two white men in the crowd. One of them was Dorothy's friend, William Smith. The dying rays of the sun fell on his hair, burnishing it like gold. A short plump white man accompanied him. William indicated the empty cartridges scattered on the ground. "Gosh! ... Just look at those shells," he remarked. "The cartridges ricocheted all the way down here!"

His companion, who came to the shooting range every morning, began to pick them up. Tal-Betal who were constantly trailing the deodhas, whispered to each other, "She must be quite far gone with the pregnancy. People are talking."

"Whose child?"

"The jatadhari's."

"The jatadhari's?"

"Shut up."

The numbers swelled. The boat dropped anchor.

The expectant crowd on the bank was startled by a wail. A strange woman tumbled off the boat. Her white hair was untied. The sendur bindi on her forehead was smeared. Her chadar was slipping off her shoulders. She knelt down and beat her forehead on the holy ground of Kamakhya, "Oh Ma! Forgive me for this great sin." She broke into a high pitched lament. "Mother, she would eat neither a morsel nor drink a drop of water the past month. We are prostitutes from Shekhadari – but we did not force her into our trade. She came to us herself. She just cries over and over again, My buffalo has been sacrificed. My buffalo has been sacrificed."

The pilgrims murmured.

"Who is that in the boat?"

The woman rolled on the ground, beating her breasts. "Ma! I could not carry the burden if she died."

The jatadhari and a few students climbed aboard the boat. The crowd gasped. A body!

The jatadhari said, "Bidhibala!"

"Bidhibala!"

"Bidhibala?"

"Yes. She is dead. It's possible she was still alive when they started out."

Nobody spoke.

The prostitutes' wailing rent the skyline.

No one really noticed when Ratnadhar came to sit by the sacrificial altar. Bidhibala's body still lay outside. Many thought it was too late to inform her family in Sualkuchi.

A priest observed, "Her father, Singhadatta will surely not be willing to perform the last rites for a daughter who has been associated with the North Shekhadri women. Do whatever needs to be done, but do it fast."

Finally, a young boy from a family of devotees with the same lineage was asked to perform the last rites. The boy sprinkled water on her ashes and collected the bones. All this while Ratnadhar sat weeping by the sacrificial altar. "Bidhibala is dead! Bidhibala is dead! Who killed her?"

The altar was wet with the blood of animals recently offered to the Goddess Manasa. Ratnadhar struck his head against it. "Bidhibala, they made a sacrifice of you instead of the buffalo," he wailed.

The month-long Manasa puja was coming to a close. The deodhas danced on. Devotees waited on the sidelines, chillums ready. The deodhas took a few puffs now and again before rejoining the dancers. Devotees sprang out of their way to avoid being trampled.

Ratnadhar's lamentations carried over all the noise. A man who had spent his last rupee on animal offerings to the goddess stood near the sacrificial altar. "My land is gone! My house is gone! I cannot educate my sons. I am bankrupt."

A priest who was assisting the deodhas, heard him. "You wicked sinner," the priest snarled. "I will smash your head to a pulp with this stick. Get out!"

Meanwhile, the priests stood around the sacrificial altar watching Ratnadhar. They looked like wild predators, waiting to pounce. "Remove the wretched creature," one of them shouted. "You boys, go and call Manomohan. Take him away."

By then, Ratnadhar was drenched in the blood of sacrifice. He lay there, clinging to the altar. Two boys tried prising him off. The numbers of goats and doves, brought for sacrifice, grew. Tal-Betal appeared out of nowhere and tugged at his arms. Ratnadhar's screams rent both heaven and hell. "Bidhibala! Take me with you. Bidhibala ... Bidhibala!"

On the second day, the deodhas were fed by five kumaris. Then they began their frenzied dance. A mountain of beheaded doves and goats rose before the Goddess Manasa. The deodhas made their way to Lord Shiva's temple to be costumed. The temple was set in a grove of ou, sonaru and peepal trees – there to be costumed. There was a motley crowd, their clothes filthy, covered in sendur, phaku powder and sweat. Even their hair was smeared with sendur and phaku powder. The chests and faces of some were stained with sacrificial blood. Barefoot they danced along, short, tall, young, old, heavy set, slim, they moved in step, dove feathers flying. Down the narrow path they went, cutting through the shrubbery like a host of evil spirits. The crowds had gathered to watch, lining the verandas of the priests' houses, calling excitedly to each other.

The floor of the Shiva temple was covered with articles of veneration. Garlands of flowers, sendur, hair oil and headdresses of wood apple leaves. New sets of clothes were laid out on plantain leaves. The deodhas gathered at the steps leading to the crumbling roof of the temple. A priest lurched up to the first one, to wash his feet. Shining bronze pitchers had been kept in readiness. He washed away the blood, sendur, phaku powder from the feet of Kuber's deodha. Then he took off his gamocha to wipe them. An angry shout of protest interrupted his ministrations. Shiva's deodha ran up, screaming abuse. "How dare you dress Kuber's deodha before the deodha of Shiva! You will die. The next seven generations of your progeny will rot in hell." Tradition ordained that Bhairava's deodha must always be costumed first.

The crowd moaned. "A terrible lapse! How could this happen?"

The priest lay at the deodha's feet, begging forgiveness. Devotees sang hymns in praise of Shiva and the goddess. Shiva's deodha eventually capitulated. The women entered the temple, singing praises to Lord Shiva. A trident was stuck near the door to the spacious hall. The floor had been swept and swabbed. Earthen lamps and incense sticks were lit.

After a while the deodhas came out of the temple in their finery, dancing to the women's songs. Their bodies, freshly daubed with sendur and oil, glistened in the light of the earthen lamps. They wore garlands of flowers and tulsi leaves on their necks and heads. The women sang on, clapping their hands to the beat.

"Hail Kali. Hail Tara, Chhinnamasta, Bagala."

The drums throbbed. Bagala's deodha bowed before the trident. He was thin as a reed, with a complexion the colour of old earthenware. Ma Tara's deodha followed, young and lithe, a garland of white karabi flowers around his neck, a wreath of tulsi leaves on his head. Then came Kuber's brawny deodha, dressed in purple robes, keeping in step with the frenetic beat.

A hush fell over the crowd as the next one appeared. Six foot tall, bony hands and feet, skin, dark as the night. It was whispered that he had drunk more blood than any of the others. The drums picked up. The women began their distinctive wailing. Kali's deodha flicked his long tongue, red with the blood from the sacrifices of last night. Raising his arms, head bowed, he began to dance. Now and again he cast an eye on the assembled devotees. His glance filled their hearts with terror.

More deodhas came out. Eyes closed, they looked like they were floating in the air. As if their movements were controlled by some ethereal power. They appeared to do nothing of their own volition. Every action seemed to be instructed by the goddess.

The deodhas lined up to move towards the goddess in the amphitheatre. Earlier they had sat on plantain leaves to be rubbed down with butter and sendur. Now their bare bodies gleamed. The deodhas of Ganesha and of Shiva, danced ahead of the others. The temple midgets broke into a run to keep pace with them.

People had come from Natpara, Hemtala, Bezpara, Napitpara, Malipara, the north and south banks. The priests' families joined the procession.

Earthen lamps glittered on the deodhas' heads. A pretty woman stood there waiting to ask Kali's deodha about her future. Her chubby little daughter was in her arms. She had a kid goat with her, for sacrifice. In all the jostling, the goat vomited. Someone next to her remarked, "That's a suckling baby you've got there. It's throwing up milk. Why have you brought it to quench the deodha's thirst?" The woman, disconcerted, looked away. The child looked at her face and then down at the animal. "Where has this goat's mummy gone?" She asked her mother.

The deodhas proceeded towards the temple.

By afternoon, red clouds had come out to nuzzle the rain clouds hanging over the holy abode. It was as if a sacrificial buffalo with its sendur smeared forehead, and garland of red hibiscus, was trying to escape into the dark bosom of the storm clouds. From the temple complex, the shrieks of the deodhas came intermittently, drowning out the trumpeting of wild elephants in the forest.

Dorothy Brown's boat appeared on the horizon. Her arrival was a point of hot discussion at the police station, among the white men who came for shooting practice, at the church, and even in the common room of the Curzon Hall in Cotton College where they had gathered during recess.

A big crowd had turned up to greet her. Dorothy's friend, William had come early. He found a place to sit on the embankment. He had completed the work Dorothy had entrusted him with. He would do anything for Dorothy. William was watching the boats through his binoculars. Every once in a while he glanced up at the sky, running his fingers through his hair.

No, the jatadhari had not come. William had heard of the frantic preparations for the meeting at which the petition to stop animal sacrifice would be presented to the chief priest. The numbers joining their lobby were heartening. More and more signature-books were piling up at the Darbhanga House.

In this British state, the head priest of the temple selected the chief priest. The British had never ever interfered. Even if there were instances of corruption, they were confined to the files of the white officials. But what about the huge mountain of signatures? Their presence was so potent, no one could possibly feign ignorance. A mercy appeal had to be the solution. Even the white men could not ignore the anguished pleas of those who had come forward to wash away the stains of blood.

The jatadhari's disciples had any number of papers and documents in their possession. In 1842, officers of the government were prohibited from interfering in the management of the temple. A directive was issued to the collector, instructing that in case of future disputes, the ordinary courts of law would determine the right of succession.

Yes, of course the matter might ultimately have to be referred to the courts of law!

One by one, a number of white men gathered on the quay. The onlookers were none too clear about what they were doing there. Was it to protect Dorothy Brown from some vague yet very real threat? Or was there some other reason?

Many had in fact seen how the police had chased the Deodhwani volunteers. But what had brought this assortment of white men to this particular place at this particular time?

The sendur smeared buffalo-clouds faded from the skyline. The boatmen's lilting song came floating over the water, to the accompaniment of the splash of oars.

Lay down your own skin on this path.
Light up your heart with that earthen lamp,
Light up the wick with your blood,
Tarry! For she would come,
She would come ...

What a song! The prostitutes from North Shekhadari sang such songs. Two drummers, squatting on the ground, hugging their knees, watched the goings on. They wore loose fitting vests over grimy dhutis. The drummer from Dotkuchi observed sagely, "The foreign woman has chosen our man and come into our fold."

The other drummer who was from Satgharia in Darrang district retorted, "So what? Haven't the white men been dragging away our girls? I used to sing the Bamun Para geet and Hyder Gazir geet on this very boat."

"Really?"

"I most certainly did. Listen: A young brahmin from downstream Brahmaputra went to Upper Assam. There he earned two pitchers of coins for performing the religious rites. He married a local girl. She was the very incarnation of a nymph. On their way home, the brahmin and his bride bought tickets on the streamer. That is where their problems began."

The drummer from Satgharia chimed in, "He looked to the east, to the west, north and south. His eyes fell on the brahmin woman from the west ... the white man could not drag his eyes away. Going down on deck, the white man tracked down his attendants. He told them to take note of his wishes – kill the brahmin and bring me his wife."

The drummer from Dotkuchi sang, "Did the white man commit the cardinal sin of killing a brahmin?"

"The attendants said that they would rather rot in hell. They would not kill a brahmin."

"So, what did the white man say?"

"He jingled some coins with the queen's seal."

"Hai, hai!"

"They called the brahmin aside and took him to see the ship's engines."

The drummer from Satgharia changed the melody "And so they separated the brahmin from his wife. They shoved him in the coal store and covered him up with coal!"

"And then?"

"Then what? The brahmin did not return. His wife wept inconsolably. The white man came and asked her, what her husband looked like."

The drummer from Satgharai picked up the tune, "Sir, my husband had six toes on his left foot."

"The white man showed her a charred foot with six toes next to the engine room. The brahmin woman saw the charred six-toed foot. She fainted. Right into the white man's arms!"

"Oh no! The white man's arms?"

"Yes, and he made her his wife on that very day."

William and the other Britishers were clustered together. They heard the sound of the boat scraping against land. Dorothy Brown emerged from under the canopy. She looked up at the sky. The red clouds were back, playing with the rain clouds.

"William!" Dorothy's face lit up. She extended her hand. William waded into the water, shoes and all. Her hand in his, Dorothy Brown gingerly stepped off and walked ashore.

These past few months had wrought a remarkable change in Dorothy.

"Dorothy, it's good to see you again old girl. Goodness me – you've put on a bit of weight. And what on earth are you wearing? My word ... a saree! Gone quite native have we ..."

Dorothy looked up at the sky again and exclaimed, "Oh! It seems like ages since I was here last!"

She shook hands with every officer present. The students from the tol folded their hands and bowed in greeting. She hugged each one affectionately in turn.

Firmly holding on to William's hand, Dorothy pushed her way through the people and climbed up the hill barefoot. Everyone had noticed the extra inches.

When they reached the Darbhanga House, she gave a little cry of dismay. "Oh dear, empty cartridges all over the place! Is that a bullet hole in the door?"

They all stepped forward to examine the door.

"That's definitely a bullet hole."

Dorothy looked at William. "It isn't wise to practice shooting at such close range."

The Englishmen nodded in agreement. Meanwhile, the students set down Dorothy Brown's luggage on the veranda.

Dorothy unlocked the door. "Oh! Those must be Ratnadhar's paintings."

Although it was not quite dark as yet, a student went off to fetch an earthen lamp. The light fell on Ratnadhar's depiction of

King Rudrasingha's body laid out on the boat, the three dancing girls, crushed to death by his side.

Dorothy invited the white men in. Proudly, she showed them the painting. "King Rudrasingha sacrificed twenty thousand buffaloes to propitiate the Goddess Durga and flooded this holy abode with blood. The valiant King Rudrasingha! Look at the painting!" She stopped abruptly. "I heard about Ratnadhar. He was moved to the hospital last night."

A tear slid down her cheek.

"Oh Ma! Will I lose the boy? Ma, will he die?"

The white men were at a loss. William pulled a kerchief from his pocket and handed it to Dorothy. "There, there." He said, trying to console her. "Chin up, old girl. He's going to be alright."

Dorothy continued bravely, "Look, how carefully he keeps the exercise books with the signatures. He hasn't left out a single person in the north and south banks."

The dam burst. Her tears blotted the pages.

William said gently, "Don't worry. I have already had a word with the district sub-judge. I have also spoken to two native munshis who fiercely oppose the sacrifices. Listen, I have other things to talk to you about. Come on, let's sit out on the veranda."

The student lit up a lamp and placed it on the veranda. Dorothy's countenance brightened.

There was a question in every one's heart.

Should William ask her directly?

Or would somebody else broach the subject?

Was Dorothy carrying the jatadhari's child?

Apparently the white men had come up here to find out the truth.

A strident cry floated to them from the distance. The deodhas. They would now prostrate themselves before the goddess. After that each would depart to his own temple.

No, they could not ask the question out loud. If there was one among them who had been sent here by Dorothy's husband, he held his tongue.

A chill ran up William's spine. He knew just how vicious Henry Brown could be. Brown would rip the jatadhari's child from Dorothy's womb and grind it into the earth with his boots.

A hermit from Gaur was singing:
Mother, you will come, you must
surely come ...

The blood from your womb spawns
myriad forms of life.
The milk from your breast
makes life immortal.
Mother, I know that you will come by this path
Where this fair skin of my body I will lay down ...

From the early morning, swarms of devotees had been heading towards this holy abode. Today was the last day of the Deodhwani.

A student from the tol who was sleeping on the floor of the Chhinnamasta temple woke with a start. He had been studying the *Kalika Purana* the previous night. The worshipper who tears the neck of an animal or bird with his bare hands commits a cardinal sin equivalent to killing a brahmin. He suffers unbearable pain.

Today the deodha would dance on the edge of an unsheathed sabre on the very floor of the goddess' abode and drink the blood of a dove, the symbol of peace.

When the student walked down to the river to bathe, he came across a group of white men who had come to the woods for shooting practice. He had never seen so many white men gathered here before.

The guns boomed. Last night a group of devotees who had come up for the Deodhwani festivities told of how volunteers had assaulted a white man on the shipping embankment.

The student ran in his wet clothes to report what was happening to the jatadhari. He was very afraid.

A crowd had gathered in front of the Chhinnamasta temple. The date for presenting the petition had been fixed. Would the white men call in the police? There was talk among the students. Everyone knew that the white men would not interfere in the internal affairs of the temple. But if someone got hurt? It would be wise to seek help.

The student stood at the entrance to the jatadhari's cave. The ascetic was meditating. He saw the silhouette in the light of the lamp hanging at the entrance. There seemed to be an aura around him. A snake was entwined in his dreadlocks. Alarmed, the boy went back and told the devotees sitting outside. But they knew already.

Blood and sweat slithered down the backs of the dancing deodhas. The tempo rose. The steps grew frenetic. The forecourts of the goddess shuddered. The floors were strewn with flowers, blood and droplets of sweat. Occasionally, a devotee would roll manically at the feet of a deodha, compelling the dancer to acknowledge his presence. Wiping the sweat from his bare back with a few wood apple leaves, the deodha would shove it into the devotee's begging hands and resume dancing.

"O Mai! O Mai!"

Kali's deodha, his tongue lolling out, danced furiously with a black goat on his back. A murmur rose: "Will he eat it raw?"

Dorothy Brown, draped in a saffron saree, stood near Kautilinga. A thin student from the tol was with her. She had spent a long time with the jatadhari, and now spoke fluent Asomiya.

A devotee in red robes had been down to the river to collect water. He turned his face away from Dorothy, emptying his pitcher, and went back to the river. Dorothy and the boy knew why. The sight of an untouchable white woman had sullied his soul.

They climbed the hill.

"We should submit our memorandum in a day or two."

Dorothy wasn't really listening. She seemed deep in thought. She was radiant in the morning light, like a nymph surfacing from the water. She had filled out, and looked more beautiful than ever. People were talking.

Dorothy gazed into the sparkling waters of the Brahmaputra. "The jatadhari read tantras to me while we travelled to North Shekhadari. He read me some lovely stories too. I can read the Asomiya script now. Did you know that in some bygone era the nymph Mahoharu, who was also known as Kunkawati, a celestial courtesan, was cursed and sent down to earth. Her descendants, the Soumars, once ruled over Kamrup ... Now

I can read them myself. Have you heard the tale of conceit?"
She chattered on.

The student from the tol listened in astonishment. He had
not been prepared to listen to Dorothy's tales, concentrating as
he was on moving her to a safer place. Only today, the body of
a white man that had floated down the Brahmaputra had been
discovered, lodged in some rocks. The Britishers who came for their
practice down below had gathered around the dead body swearing
vengeance. "The deodhas will soon begin their sword dance and
drink raw blood," he said tersely. "I shall take you up the hill. No
one will find you there."

Dorothy looked at him. The student had never before seen
such eyes. They seemed to embrace the sky. The jatadhari's eyes
were deep set. He had overheard someone saying that the ascetic's
eyes were like burning pyres. Poets say that only those with fire in
their eyes can change this world.

In front of the amphitheatre, in the forecourts of the temple,
the deodhas danced to the pounding rhythm of the drums.
Their eyes drooped from intoxication. Still, they showed no sign
of fatigue.

In a short while, the sacred abode of the goddess was packed
to capacity. Today the deodhas would dance on the blades of
their swords.

Dorothy Brown and the student climbed up the hill in search of
a secure location. They came across two men grinding spices in
front of a deserted house.

"Grinding spices at this hour?" the student asked.

"Yes, we have to leave early tomorrow. Those goats tethered there are for sacrifice. We won't have time to grind the spices later."

Dorothy saw the goats grazing close by, oblivious to their fate. Flecks of powdered spice spattered their bodies. Grabbing the student's hand, she quickened her pace.

It had begun to rain. The deodhas continued their dance. Kali's deodha with the protruding tongue danced harder than any other. Someone clung to his feet, demanding to know his future. The deodha dragged the man all over the floor.

None seemed tire. They had lost count of the clanging bells, of day and night.

The jatadhari had come to Dorothy's room that morning, before sitting down to meditate. "Don't go out! The white men's guards are all over the place, hunting down the freedom fighters. The enemies' fingernails are sharp. Their teeth are like razors. Be careful."

With those words, he had taken his leave. "Ma! Ma! Ma! You are glorious in your own blood, Ma! Adorn yourself in robes of flowers."

Accompanied by the students of the tol who had come to put their signatures on the memorandum, the jatadhari took the narrow path down to that part of the river where very few dared venture. The depth here was almost unfathomable. There were stories of women from the almost extinct Brahma clan committing sati in this part of the river.

Disregarding the jatadhari's warnings, Dorothy had come with the student to watch the dance.

They heard the primal cries of animals being slaughtered!

The student said, "We shouldn't be standing here. Someone seems to have been wounded."

"Wounded?"

"Yes."

Dorothy did not move. Mesmerized, she watched the dance. She stood under a wood apple tree. She wouldn't be visible from below.

"What are these marks on the trees?"

"Targets for the white man's shooting sessions. Here are the empty cartridges."

"The wood apple tree has been wounded! Jatadhari says that the wood apple tree is the embodiment of Shiva's matted tresses."

"Yes," the student added, "And the three leaves of the wood apple tree are the three Vedas – Rig, Yajur and Sama."

She had heard many stories from the banks of the Brahmaputra during her sojourn with the jatadhari.

A devotee performing Chandika worship with a garland of lotus flowers earns a place in the abode of the Sun God. Offer a house of flowers to Ma Kamakhya and her blessings will provide you with all worldly pleasures and secure your place in the abode of Durga. One who worships the goddess with a thousand karabi flowers and a thousand kundu flowers will find all his desires satisfied and all his wishes fulfilled.

Why isn't Nilachal flooded with flowers?

The shrieks of the devotees reached fever pitch. The priests completed their veneration of the Goddess Manasa and brought out the sacrificial machete. A current of anticipation trilled through the crowd. Like a hissing serpent. Four men formed a square and lifted the machete on their shoulders. Kali's mount jumped up on the blade. The applause was thunderous.

Dorothy Brown's eyes welled up.

What will he do? Firmly holding onto the student's hand, Dorothy watched, appalled. A devotee pushed through the crowd and offered a dove to the deodha. He tore off its neck with his teeth and drank the blood, then threw the carcass into the crowd.

Oh no. No! Such things must not happen! The jatadhari had said that a devotee who kills animals and birds with his bare hands commits a cardinal sin, equal to killing a brahmin.

"Ma ... Ma ... Ma!"

It was the jatadhari's voice. A cry of distress ...

Sunshine filtered through the clouds, like liquid gold mixed with blood and water, flooding the sacred abode. A tantrik once said, "Ma's womb must always be filled with blood. Only then will the world survive."

Still, disciples seeking the loving bounty of the Ma's heart kept chanting the Mahakali shlokas given to them by the Mahadev.

"Ma! The brightness of your face surpasses the brilliance of the sun and the moon. Your feet are the epitome of kindness. Ma, countless molten moons find refuge in your face."

She had learned so much from the jatadhari. Letting down his guard, he had once even mentioned that he had studied history. He had lived in a mysterious cave in the Vindhyas – the Central Indian mountain range separating the wide northern plains from the south – for a period, after renouncing worldly pleasures. He had come to this sacred abode of the goddess with a team of tantriks from North Kashi.

One night he had woken up to the sound of clicking hooves. He had followed the buffalo being dragged to its doom. It was a horrific tug-of-war. The buffalo had defecated. Its frightened eyes seemed to bore into his heart, just as a child would find its way to its mother's bosom. He had returned from the sacrificial altar a changed man. The echo of its hooves would continually torment his soul.

"I shall stay," Dorothy had said, "I shall be your shadow forever. Our relationship cannot be defined. It is a very special bond."

A shot rang out from the forest, down below.

The student shouted, "That was a gun. Run!"

Like a vandalized minaret, Dorothy Brown's bullet ridden body rolled down the slope. The bullets ripped mercilessly into the branches of the wood apple trees.

W ho killed Dorothy Brown?

The guards tramped round the temple complex. They had no authority to enter the temple. Their heavy boots echoed in the Soubhagya Kunda. The idol of the Goddess Manasa had been immersed. Banana trees, flowers, the goddess's face and silk garb floated like debris from a sunken boat.

The white soldiers marched up to the young girl students who were offering water to the deodhas. It was the water offering festival. Tender coconuts, succulent fruits, sweets and bowls filled with sacrificial blood were laid out for each deodha. Everyone sat in a circle. Two drunken devotees collapsed on the two girls. They were removed to the far end of the amphitheatre and propped upright against the walls.

As the guards marched about, devotees from the north and south banks of the Brahmaputra, the Kamakhya residents and residents of Natpara, Hemtola, Bamunpara, Bezpara, and Malipara followed them wherever they went, stirring up a big commotion.

At the Bhairavi tank, the turtles soaking up the sun on the bank scuttled back into the pond in alarm. A devotee remarked, "When Gadadhar Singha was on the run, he was protected by the goddess. He was so cleverly hidden by a branch of that banyan tree that the Ahom King's sleuths couldn't trace him."

Another disciple chimed in, "King Gadadhar could eat a whole buffalo by himself!"

"Quiet!" Others hissed. "Shut up!"

The soldiers were searching the places where human sacrifice was once said to have been performed. Someone whispered that the soldiers had come to seek blessings and adorn themselves with amulets.

The white men's soldiers tramped past the sacrificial altar. Since they couldn't go inside the temple, they tried peering in from the outside.

A devotee shouted, "If you see a woman in blood coloured robes, think about the Goddess Bhairavi. Tripura Bhairavi, the goddess who is thrice terrible, wears red robes and has four arms. She carries a book in her left hand. Garlands of skulls adorn her head, breasts and hips. It says so in the texts."

The soldiers turned their attention to the drummers' camps. Most of the drummers were sleeping after three days of non-stop drumming and large doses of opium. The soldiers rummaged through their clothes and utensils, startling them out of their slumber with the tips of their bayonets.

The chief constable, who had been overseeing the proceedings from a distance, now headed down the jungle path. One of the soldiers discovered a cache of empty cartridges under a bhatghila bush. More soldiers came. They began cutting away the foliage, looking for empty shells. Tal and Betal led them to places where they were shocked by the sheer number of spent bullets.

When the soldiers entered the Darbhanga House, one of the midgets said, "This is where Mistress Dorothy fell."

His twin added, "The student dragged her all the way here. His desperate screams brought people rushing in. They stood right there. Those are her blood stains."

A very short devotee got up and pointed them out for the soldiers. The crowd was silent. Some of the soldiers went into the rooms and rummaged through the neat stacks of signature-books. The students following behind them protested.

"What are you doing? These are ...!"

"Shut up!" The soldiers growled.

Many students had signed in their own blood. How could their compatriots stand by and watch!

The soldiers pulled out Dorothy Brown's two trunks and rummaged through her clothes hoping to find something – letters, a revolver! Her nightclothes frilled with lace. Chintz dresses, silk lingerie. Various pairs of canvas shoes. A gaily printed parasol. Hats.

The numbers grew. They hung around Darbhanga House examining the rusty bloodstains. The two midgets chorused, "Who killed her? Who killed her?"

The soldiers took Ratnadhar's paintings out into the light, hoping to find some clue. They studied each one carefully, then flung it back into the room.

The students were hysterical. "Ratnadhar is in the hospital. Careful!"

The midgets joined them, "Careful!"

As their protests grew louder, onlookers warned the midgets, "They will break your bones with their batons!"

The soldiers lurked around the premises for a while longer. They stood in front of the temple of Chhinnamasta and stared into its mysterious recesses. In the gloom they could make out sacrificial blood in a copper plate. They stepped back. A government directive prohibited their entry into the temples.

The soldiers marched on to where the Britishers held their target practice. They combed the area for clues. The Gurkha guard brought them a massive register. The chief constable opened the book and went through the names. There were many names. Names of seven officials from the Revenue Department, beginning with Peter Warner; four officials from the Survey of India, led by Harold Henry Creed. New names from the Income Tax department – Sidney John, Paul Brighton, Hill Smith, Raghubir Chowdhury, Bishnupada Sen, Joseph Kilar, and Robert Hine. The list also included the names of two notorious sons of a now retired official of the Assam Bengal Railway – Dante and Alexander. Another retired official, Montgomery, of the Goyanand Postal Ferry Service was also on the list. Sweeping aside the empty bottles with his baton, the chief constable ordered, "Search the place."

One particular name had leapt out of that long register.

At once the soldiers began to rifle through the tents. The chief lost no time working out the angles from which the shots could have been fired. The bullets could hit her from various positions. The mystery of the heap of empty shells they had found was solved. Dorothy's husband had been there yesterday evening, at exactly this time.

Meanwhile, the sun was setting. Red clouds were reflected on the Brahmaputra like blood on the water.

The jatadhari had spent the entire night at the Bharalu Police station. When they finally let him go, he went back to his own cave accompanied by students from the tol and a group of devotees. His eyes were like drops of sacrificial blood. The rusty dreadlocks were plastered to his back.

At times, tears seemed to well up in his eyes. At others, fires burned in them. Most of the time, he walked with his eyes closed. He was familiar with the byways of the sacred abode. Occasionally he would cry, "O no! No! Ma ... Ma ... Ma ..."

His fists were clenched. His breathing was shallow. He was unable to come to terms with Dorothy's murder. He had renounced the world. Still he found it difficult to accept that she was gone. His cries of anguish shook the very foundations of the goddess' abode.

There had been a lathi-charge at the police station. Followers of the jatadhari, angry that their mentor had been taken into custody, had pelted stones at the doors and windows. A few students had to be hospitalized. Even some bystanders were hurt.

The procession moved along, the jatadhari in the lead. Today they would assemble at the platform of the Soubhagya Kunda and most humbly present their petition.

The jatadhari marched on. The man was once a student of history at the Benaras Hindu University. He had roamed around North Kashi for a while after his initiation as an ascetic. Later on he had meditated for a long time in a cave in the Vindhyas. It was said that during this period he had lived at one with nature.

Venemous serpents had nested in his matted locks. Wild birds had perched on his arms.

Respectful of all creatures, the jatadhari could not bear the sight of blood at the goddess' sacred abode. He would say, "Man is god's creation. Man has many a thing to learn from animals. Only when men and animals live in harmony will the world become a paradise."

The British police officers had interrogated the jatadhari through the night.

"Who killed Dorothy Brown?"

"Her husband?"

"Or some devotees?"

"Or priests?"

"Or nationalist volunteers?"

"Or soldiers?"

"Or was it one of the white men aiming bullets?"

"Was she carrying your child?"

"Where have you come from? What sort of initiation? Do you have any papers?"

The jatadhari said nothing.

The procession grew in size. After some time he entered the cave. A group of tantriks and priests waited for the jatadhari near the Soubhagya Kunda. Certainly something was about to happen today. The veneration at the temple was over for the day. The doors were already closed.

A couple of men were making arrangements to carry away the carcass of a huge buffalo that had just been slaughtered. It appeared as if the bleeding had stopped, but as they moved the animal, red drops began to spill from it.

An awning had been erected near the Soubhagya Kunda. People were pouring in through all four of the temple's gateways.

Everyone was there – descendants of Kashyap family, the norm setters; the performing line of the Bhargavs – the Mudiyars, storekeepers, attendants, their children. Even two machete men were standing beside the altar. They were dressed in red dhutis and half sleeved shirts. Their documents were in their pockets.

The assembly waited. The jatadhari would come – a venomous serpent riding in his dreadlocks. He would present a petition to the chief priest today. It would usher in a new era. The goddess would be venerated with flowers.

A petition. An impassioned plea. Written with the blood of the Ma's devotees. A young student from the tol on the south bank carried the petition on a salver on his head. He walked ahead of the jatadhari. He was very light skinned.

The young man was well built. His hair was thick as a beehive. The golden ring tied to his sacred thread glinted beneath his silk shawl. The goddess was believed to favour kunda, bakul and bel leaves. The young man marched ahead confidently, with garlands of the fragrant flowers and a petition beautifully inscribed in the Asomiya script. The band of devotees walked behind the jatadhari.

After Dorothy Brown's death, the jatadhari had taken a vow of silence. A brace of drummers representing the Karkabari Orput performers were in the procession. Their rhythm was like the buffalo hoof beats in the dead of night.

Today the jatadhari was dressed in red robes, like the tantriks. The midgets trotted at his side. Every now and again they would step out of the procession and like monkeys, shin up the imli and bhatghila trees that lined the path. Everyone watched their antics. None commented. They walked ahead in silence.

Where had all these tantriks come from? They were standing near the store and the bell house. A couple of them had matted locks. Most of them were clean. Their complexions were like dried reeds. Curiosity was apparent on their faces.

A tantrik suddenly appeared before them – it was as if he rose from a ditch under a broken post. His face was partially covered with a cloth towel. The same dried-reed complexion. His face was dirty. Its expression vicious likes a serpent about to strike.

The students whispered, agitated: "That tantrik drinks the blood of slaughtered animals. He took the river route to this holy abode of the goddess. No one knows him. He rubs his body with blood instead of ashes from the sacred pits."

The tantrik shrieked, "You fools! The Goddess Kamakhya has quenched her thirst for thousands of years with blood of both humans and animals. Haven't you heard that Ganesha is venerated with liquor, Vishnu with clarified butter, Shiva with music, and Chandika with blood? Are you not familiar with the intricacies of tantrik ritual? You dare to change the practice of millennia! You will rot. Rot in hell!"

The boy carrying the garland bedecked petition was perplexed for a moment. He stepped back. Chhinnamasta Jatadhari commanded, "Carry on."

The students from the tol chorused, "Move along, move along."

Everyone looked ahead and saw the chief priest waiting patiently. He did not stand with the other priests. He stood near the sacrificial altar.

The crowd was growing steadily. Once again the tantrik slithered out from the cracks of a tumbled-down monument, like a poisonous serpent of doom. He stood near the sacrificial altar and shrieked, "What are you all gaping at? Bring the machete."

An agonized call tore from the depths of the jatadhari's soul, "Ma! Ma!"

People in the procession echoed his call.

The brahmin student from the tol placed the petition before the chief priest.

"Bring it. Bring the machete," the tantrik repeated.

The chief priest maintained his silence. He was a handsome man. His complexion was like old ivory. Another group of tantriks came to stand beside the first. Their red garments seemed stained with blood. Their eyes smouldered with hatred. Their faces shone like the copper vessels used for offerings of sacrificial blood.

People had come from all over – North Shekhadari, Nalbari, Palashbari, Boko, Karkabori and even Khakhapara, Khatara, Deomornoi in Darrang. The students had collected a large number of signatures from the devotees. Most of them were wretchedly poor. Their skin was dry and shrivelled. There were quite a few brahmins, pale as ivory, who had gone to Coochbehar to earn money and look for brides. Now they were old, haggard, frustrated bachelors.

The tantrik said again, "Bring the machete."

The jatadhari went up to the chief priest and directed the student who had carried the petition to read it out.

Silence.

The student, choking with emotion, read the petition out loud. The murmuring grew louder. The chief priest who had been quiet all this while raised his hand, asking for silence.

The student read on as if he were endowed with some divine power. Once the reading was over, other students went up and expressed their views.

The tantriks, scattered around the premises, began to hiss like malevolent snakes waiting to strike. A tantrik from Gaur, a Sanskrit scholar, came forward. Long hair. A cruel face, his nose sharp as a dagger. He raised his arms and spat out, "Our country's wealth has fallen into the hands of untouchables. The king is on the run, the nation is in turmoil. And you want to snatch the blood from the mouth of the goddess! Ma Tamreshwari, the Goddess Sakti's manifestation, is furious that she has been deprived of human blood. You sinners, you will burn in hell. The whole country will be razed to the ground."

A devotee from the back rows shouted, "What does the tantrik say?"

On cue, the midgets went up to the sacrificial altar and heckled, "An old bull cannot be cursed by a vulture."

All hell broke loose. A tantrik nearby grabbed Betal. He was joined by others. They beat his head against the altar. In front of everyone, they broke his skull open. The onlookers were too stunned to react.

The jatadhari's people sat in shocked silence, as the midget's broken body was dragged out of the crowd by his twin. There was however, a great deal of hissing from the other camp. As if countless sabres had been drawn at once from their scabbards.

Another tantrik called spitefully, "What would you do if we tore your petition to shreds?"

Malice flashed from his eyes.

The hissing reached a crescendo. The tantrik snarled, "The white men have interfered enough in the activities of the temple. You have made it easy for them by collecting signatures."

He glared at the jatadhari, as if waiting for a signal to pounce, to rip him apart.

The chief priest raised his hand. An eerie silence descended.

Only the wails of the grieving midget were heard in the distance. Suddenly a priest in red robes asked with relish, "You have written this in consultation with the students from the tol? You have asked why dumb harmless animals should be dragged to the altar. You have said that if it is blood that is required, devotees should offer their own. Haven't you?"

Once again there was silence.

"Since you speak of blood, let us see some proof here and now," he said in a dialect from Upper Assam.

The other tantriks in his band chorused, "The goddess is satiated for a thousand years with one human sacrifice. Devotees can earn the same benefit by offering their own blood. Now let the act commence."

A current of adrenaline shuddered through the jatadhari's followers. The shaven headed tantrik said, "The sacred texts specify that when ones own blood is offered, it must be either from below the navel or from the back. Blood from the arms or the stomach is also acceptable. O Chhinnamasta Jatadhari! Your disciples are sickly. The goddess will not accept their blood. You will have to cut a part of your own body and offer a lotus leaf cup filled with your blood. A razor, a machete, a sharp knife – you can use any of these. Remember, that the larger the blade, the more auspicious it is."

The jatadhari's followers who had worked so tirelessly to collect signatures were shaken. But only for a moment. The tantrik repeated, "You claim that a vow is more likely to be fulfilled by an offering of one's own blood rather than another's. Now prove it."

All the tantriks shrieked their hysterical agreement.

Only Tal's wailing rose over the silence. The tantriks and the priests scanned the faces of the jatadhari's followers. Just as a priest examines an animal offered for sacrifice.

The jatadhari, closed his eyes, meditating. Then he opened them and looked around. As if for the first time since Dorothy's death, his vision was clear. Sparks of fire seemed to shoot from his deep set eyes. A divine aura suffused his person.

He went forward to stand five yards from the chief priest at the sacrificial altar. All eyes were on him. His massive dreadlocks were the colour of old rusted iron. He raised his powerful arms. Like the mighty Ravana who grew in strength with every wound in battle, he drew a razor from his waistband for all to see, sliced off a piece of his own flesh from below his navel. Holding his bleeding flesh in one hand, he called, "Ma! Ma!"

Hundreds of devotees standing behind him chorused, "Ma! Ma! Ma!" The sky above the holy abode resounded with their cry. The doves plastered to the walls of the temple rose in a flurry. Students from the tol stepped forward. With the same weapon, the youths began to cut flesh from their bodies. They continued through the night. The sacrificial altar was drenched in the blood of young men.

People stared in horror as blood flowed in the sacred abode of the goddess until after midnight.

Towards early dawn, the clouds burst. The rain came down. It carried away the raw blood with all the other rubbish and swept it into the bosom of the Brahmaputra.

In the morning, the sun rose once more. In the clear light of day, no one could see a trace of blood. Not a single bloodstain remained.

BIO NOTES

Indira Goswami, also known as Mamoni Raisom Goswami, has written several novels, hundreds of short stories and a number of research papers. Her works have been extensively translated into various bhashas including English. Several feature films, television serials, telefilms and stage plays have been adapted from her novels and short stories.

Recipient of the International Tulsi Award on the occasion of International Conference on "Tulsi Das and His Works" from the Florida International University, Florida, USA, she has also been honoured with several national and international awards. These include the Jnanpith Award, Sahitya Akademi Award, Bharat Nirman Award, Assam Sahitya Sabha Award, Katha Award for Creative Fiction, the Kamal Kumari Foundation Award and the International Jury Award for the film *Adarya* based on her novel *Une Khowa Hawda*.

A trained metallurgical engineer in Guwahati, **Prashant Goswami** is a writer and translator. He translates from Asomiya to English.

The winner of the
HUTCH CROSSWORD BOOK AWARD 2005
for Indian Language Fiction Translation

Katha Hindi Library
ISBN: 978-81-87649-54-0
Price: 250

"Krishna Sobti's *The Heart Has Its Reasons (Dil-o-Danish)* is a subtle and penetrating chronicle of human emotions. The story centres upon three characters, a man and two women. All three are drawn from established types of a particular age and society; yet Sobti endows them with rare individuality and brings them to vivid and particular life. And beyond all particularities, their interaction opens up the general working of the human heart, its intricate effect on relationships and social structures, and the unfolding of a person's self-knowledge. Both male and female sensibilities are rendered with equal insight and empathy. Thus Sobti infuses new meaning even into the familiar aphorism of the novel's title in translation ..."

Shah Abdul Latif

why search everywhere?
nearer than your breath is he
just remove the screen
between you and him

Known as one of the greatest sufi works in history, Shah
Abdul Latif's Shah Jo Risalo is a prayer, a cry for the beloved.
Written more than 250 years ago, Latif's poetry is deeply
rooted in the human experience of searching for the self – a
self that is one with the nirakaar, the omnipresent, centered
within yet diffuse as attar. Katha proudly presents the first
ever English translation of the Risalo in India.

Katha Asia Library/Katha
Poets Cafe
ISBN: 978-81-89020-54-5
Price: 350

Arumugam

A timeless tale of a child denied his chidhood; Arumugam explores the relationship between a mother and son, the difficult emotions that weave their stories into a single fabric of love. Thrown from a secure, loving home into the cruel world of the Chekkumedu prostitutes, Arumugam learns that his perceptions of life are as unreal as wisps of smoke and understands in the end, that the only truth is the voice of a loving heart.

Expertly translated by D Krishna Ayyar, Katha presents one of the finest contemporary writers in Tamil.

"Imayam is one of the first Tamil writers to bring the Dalits to life through his exquisite novels ..."

- Sundara Ramaswamy

Katha Tamil Library
ISBN: 978-81-87649-27-4
Price: 300

Remembering Amma

A moment of insight is all it takes to topple a goddess from her pedestal. To Appu, a Vedic scholar, his mother is as pure and beautiful as the scriptures he has been studying. Yet when he discovers his idol's feet of clay, he returns to the sanctuary of his padasalai, only to be drawn into a perilous relationship with the young widow, Indu.

Thi Jaa weaves a lyrical story of a vedapadasalai by the Kaveri and an orthodox household in Madras with an array of vivid, lifelike characters. His portrayal of women who pursue their passions with calm self-assurance is bold and uncritical.

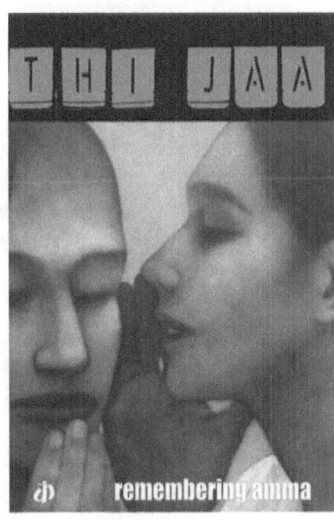

Katha Tamil Library
ISBN: 978-81-87649-31-1
Price: 200

Help shape my future!

doctor, engineer, policewoman, mechanic, computer specialist...

What will I be?

What happens when 1300 children, a determined Katha team of teachers and activists, and a whole community come together? Yes ... Sheer magic! You'll find this excitement in the air when you enter our school, a brick low-cost building.

We, the children and women of Govindpuri and Changlang in Arunachal Pradesh, a large slum cluster of more than 1,50,000 people, have come a long way in more than fourteen years with Katha. But there are excitements ahead. Small but sure steps towards self-confidence, self-reliance touched by the power of self-esteem. Many of us are working today to support our families in ways we could never have dreamt of! Many of us have finished our BAs and BComs from Delhi's colleges. We once didn't even dare to dream ... today dreams are coming true, we talk of what Katha's goal of an uncommon education for a common good can help us all achieve. We are fun-loving dreamers-doers at Katha. And we'd like you to join us in our fight against poverty.

Be our special friend! Sponsor quality education at Katha. Giving has never been so easy, or with so much impact. It costs you just Rs 250/month to provide basic quality education to one of us. That's Rs 3,000/yr. Include computer education for a child with just Rs 1,800/yr more!

Please send your cheque/DD in favour of Katha Resources to Educate a Child (REACH) Fund to **Katha, A3, Sarvodaya Enclave, Sri Aurobindo Marg, New Delhi 110017**. For more details visit us at **www.katha.org**. Or write to us at **donorrelation@katha.org**.

Donations to Katha Reach Fund qualify for 100% tax exemption under 80G of the IT Act. Registered under FCRA, Katha can receive donations in foreign currencies.